Murder at Pope Investigations

A Sand and Sea Mystery

by

Kathi Daley

Books by Kathi Daley
Come for the murder, stay for the romance.

Zoe Donovan Cozy Mystery:
Halloween Hijinks
The Trouble With Turkeys
Christmas Crazy
Cupid's Curse
Big Bunny Bump-off
Beach Blanket Barbie
Maui Madness
Derby Divas
Haunted Hamlet
Turkeys, Tuxes, and Tabbies
Christmas Cozy
Alaskan Alliance
Matrimony Meltdown
Soul Surrender
Heavenly Honeymoon
Hopscotch Homicide
Ghostly Graveyard
Santa Sleuth
Shamrock Shenanigans
Kitten Kaboodle
Costume Catastrophe
Candy Cane Caper
Holiday Hangover
Easter Escapade
Camp Carter
Trick or Treason
Reindeer Roundup
Hippity Hoppity Homicide

Firework Fiasco
Henderson House
Holiday Hostage
Lunacy Lake
Celtic Christmas – *December 2019*

Zimmerman Academy The New Normal
Zimmerman Academy New Beginnings
Ashton Falls Cozy Cookbook

Tj Jensen Paradise Lake Mystery:

Pumpkins in Paradise
Snowmen in Paradise
Bikinis in Paradise
Christmas in Paradise
Puppies in Paradise
Halloween in Paradise
Treasure in Paradise
Fireworks in Paradise
Beaches in Paradise
Thanksgiving in Paradise – *October 2019*

Rescue Alaska Mystery:

Finding Justice
Finding Answers
Finding Courage
Finding Christmas
Finding Shelter – *Early 2020*

Whales and Tails Cozy Mystery:

Romeow and Juliet
The Mad Catter
Grimm's Furry Tail
Much Ado About Felines
Legend of Tabby Hollow
Cat of Christmas Past
A Tale of Two Tabbies
The Great Catsby
Count Catula
The Cat of Christmas Present
A Winter's Tail
The Taming of the Tabby
Frankencat
The Cat of Christmas Future
Farewell to Felines
A Whisker in Time
The Catsgiving Feast
A Whale of a Tail
The Catnap Before Christmas – *December 2019*

Writers' Retreat Mystery:

First Case
Second Look
Third Strike
Fourth Victim
Fifth Night
Sixth Cabin
Seventh Chapter
Eighth Witness
Ninth Grave

A Tess and Tilly Mystery:
The Christmas Letter
The Valentine Mystery
The Mother's Day Mishap
The Halloween House
The Thanksgiving Trip
The Saint Paddy's Promise
The Halloween Haunting – *September 2019*

The Inn at Holiday Bay:
Boxes in the Basement
Letters in the Library
Message in the Mantel
Answers in the Attic
Haunting in the Hallway – *August 2019*
Pilgrim in the Parlor – *October 2019*
Note in the Nutcracker – *December 2019*

The Hathaway Sisters:
Harper
Harlow
Hayden – *Early 2020*

Haunting by the Sea:
Homecoming by the Sea
Secrets by the Sea
Missing by the Sea
Betrayal by the Sea
Christmas by the Sea – *Fall 2019*
Thanksgiving by the Sea – *Fall 2020*

Sand and Sea Hawaiian Mystery:
Murder at Dolphin Bay
Murder at Sunrise Beach
Murder at the Witching Hour
Murder at Christmas
Murder at Turtle Cove
Murder at Water's Edge
Murder at Midnight
Murder at Pope Investigations
Murder at Shell Beach - *Early 2020*

A Cat in the Attic Mystery:
The Curse of Hollister House – *September 2019*
The Mystery Before Christmas – *November 2019*

Seacliff High Mystery:
The Secret
The Curse
The Relic
The Conspiracy
The Grudge
The Shadow
The Haunting

Road to Christmas Romance:
Road to Christmas Past

Chapter 1

Tuesday, June 25

I should have been surprised to find the tall man with the dark skin and dark hair dead just inside the front door when I arrived at Pope Investigations, the detective agency where I work with my father, Keanu Pope, but he wasn't the first gunshot victim I'd stumbled upon this month. He was, in fact, the third. The remains of the first gunshot victim had been found on the beach behind the oceanfront condo where I live with my cousin, Kekoa. My brother, Jason, a detective for the Honolulu Police Department, figured the murder was a random act that I'd just happened to have stumbled upon. When the second body was found propped up on the lifeguard tower at the Dolphin Bay Resort, where I'd been working just one day a week since taking a full-time position at the detective agency, my brother considered that I might be connected to both men in some way. Jason learned that the first victim was a retired Air Force Master Sergeant who was vacationing on Oahu, and the second was a nightclub owner living in Honolulu. As hard as he'd tried, he hadn't been able to find a connection between the two men, or between the two men and me. After several days, he'd moved onto other theories. But now that a third victim had been found at the location where I spent the majority of my time, in my mind there was no denying that someone was leaving me bodies.

After checking for a pulse to confirm that the man was actually dead, I called Jason, who promised to come right over. I was about to walk around to the beach in order to get away from the gruesome sight when a dark four-door sedan pulled into the drive. I realized this was my first client of the day, so I took a deep breath and headed toward the car, intent on heading the woman off before she noticed the murder victim just inside the front door.

"Hokulani Palakiko?" I asked, greeting the dark-haired woman who was wearing a colorful dress in a Hawaiian print.

"Yes." The woman leaned out through her open driver's door window. "You can call me Hoku."

"My name is Lani. Lani Pope. I'm afraid we have a bit of a situation this morning, and I'm going to need to reschedule."

"Situation?" The woman looked toward the front of the building for the first time.

"We've had a breakin," I decided not to mention the dead body. "I'm so sorry for the inconvenience, but if you leave a number where you can be reached, I'll call you with a new time to meet."

The woman furrowed her brow. "You do understand that my husband is missing?"

I nodded. "Yes. My father filled me in."

"I understand that a breakin is inconvenient, but I would think that a missing person would be a bit more of a priority."

"Yes, I see your point. It is just that the HPD officer I spoke to told me to wait for him and not to touch anything. Perhaps we can meet later today. I'm not sure if it will work to meet here at the office, but I would be willing to meet you at your home." I glanced at my watch. It was just ten o'clock now. "I should be done here by noon."

The woman frowned. She huffed out a breath, drummed her fingers on the steering wheel in front of her, and, it seemed, generally did everything she could to convey her annoyance. "Okay." She adjusted her sunglasses and turned to look directly at me. "I guess two hours won't make all that much difference, but I expect you to be prompt."

"I'll do my best."

The woman gave me her address, which luckily wasn't far from the office. I hoped she'd be long gone before Jason arrived, so I entered her phone number and home address in my phone and promised to text her with a confirmation that I would be free by twelve once I spoke to the police. She hemmed and hawed a bit more, I was sure in an effort to make certain that I understood exactly how unhappy she was with the situation, but eventually, she pulled out of the drive and headed down the highway. Minutes after she pulled away, Jason pulled into the lot in front of Pope Investigations.

I ran over to the car to greet my second oldest of five brothers. "Thank you for coming so quickly."

Jason looked toward the house. "Is Dad here?"

"He is on the South Shore this morning. I left him a message, but haven't heard back from him. I'm not exactly sure who he is meeting, but he mentioned something about a new client."

"And the victim?"

"Tall, male. Young looking, maybe mid-twenties. I'm pretty sure I don't know the man, but he does look a little familiar. I've tried to remember where I might have seen him, but I came up empty."

Jason turned as another HPD cruiser showed up. "Okay. I think it is best that you wait out here. Colin and I will have a look."

"I have to leave for another appointment at eleven-thirty. I can come back after I'm done if need be. I'm sure Dad will head over once he gets my message."

Jason nodded. "Okay. I'll come back out and talk to you once I have a chance to assess the situation. Maybe you can just wait on the lanai.

"Okay. I'll be there. If you need me, holler."

After Jason went inside, I sat down on a patio chair and checked my messages. There was one from my dentist reminding me that it was time for a checkup and cleaning; a text from my boss at the Dolphin Bay Resort where I still worked on Saturdays as a water safety officer, letting me know he had made up the schedule for the Fourth of July and that I was going to be needed for a ten hour shift; and a missed call from Dad. I opened my phone app and called him back. He picked up on the first ring.

"Hi, Dad. Did you get my message?"

"I did. Are you okay?"

"I'm fine. Jason and Colin are here. I'm waiting outside."

Dad blew out a breath loud enough for me to hear, although, without corresponding facial cues, I was unable to tell if it was a breath of relief, anxiety, or irritation.

"Three murder victims in three weeks all placed so as to make it likely that they'd be found by you is not a coincidence. I'm not liking this one bit. I think we should talk to Jason about protective custody for you."

"No, thanks," I responded immediately. "I can take care of myself."

Dad didn't argue but I had a feeling this conversation was not over.

"Is Kekoa there with you?" He asked.

Kekoa worked full-time for the Dolphin Bay Resort and part-time for us answering phones and taking care of the filing and bookkeeping.

"No. She planned to be in this afternoon. I'll call her and let her know not to bother to come in today."

"I just finished up here and am on my way back. I should be there in an hour."

"Just so you know," I added, "the new client with the missing husband you told me about showed up after I arrived but before Jason pulled in. I met her at her car and told her we'd had a breakin. I didn't mention the murder. She agreed to meet with me at her home later today since the office was unavailable. I am meeting her at noon."

"I guess that will be okay. Generally speaking, I am not a fan of you meeting clients at their homes unless I am along, but Hokulani Palakiko seems harmless enough, and I know she is concerned about her husband. I should be back by the time you return from the interview so we can discuss a strategy later this afternoon."

"Okay."

"And Lani. Be careful. I know that you are a capable young woman, but it seems as if you have somehow garnered the attention of a very dangerous person who has already killed three people and most likely won't hesitate to kill again."

"I know. I'll be careful." After I hung up with Dad, I got up from the patio chair and walked out onto the beach. I let the warm water roll over my bare feet and then called Kekoa to fill her in. I explained about the breakin and the body inside the entry and suggested she hold off coming in to take care of the bookkeeping until tomorrow. Like everyone else, she was concerned that this serial killer seemed to be focused in on me, but I assured her I would be fine and we would talk later.

Jason walked out the back door and onto the beach just as I was finishing my conversation with Kekoa. "So?" I asked.

"The victim was shot at close range with what looks to have been a small caliber handgun. We'll know more when we get the ballistics report back. It appears, based on lack of blood spatter, that the man was shot elsewhere and then dumped the same as the other two. With this third victim, I am more convinced than ever that you are somehow at the center of whatever is going on. We might want to consider protective custody. Did you get ahold of Dad?"

I nodded. "He is on his way from the South Shore, and there is no way I am going to sit around in a safe house when there is some wacko running around killing people and then leaving the remains for me like some sort of a sick gift. I need to meet with our new client, but I will come back when I'm done, and we can talk about this some more. I'm not sure what I can tell you that would help you to figure out who is doing this, but I am certain that we need to find the guy before he kills again."

"I agree. And we'll talk some more about protective custody when I am done here as well."

I was never going to agree to protective custody. I knew it, and he knew it, so I didn't bother to argue. I simply said my goodbyes and headed toward my car. Having a missing person to look for seemed like a distraction at this point, but Hoku was our client, and she was paying us good money to find her husband, who I was fairly sure she was more than just a little worried about.

I followed the directions provided by the Maps app on my phone to a large two-story house located in a nice neighborhood just a few blocks from the sea. Hoku's car was in the drive, so I pulled up on the street. One of these days, I was going to trade in my old Jeep for something that wasn't older than I was, but I never seemed to have enough income to deal with car payments, so a new car would need to wait.

I walked up the shrub-lined walkway toward the covered porch. I rang the bell and then waited.

"Oh good, you came," the woman said, stepping aside. "Is your father with you?"

"He couldn't make it, but he does plan to consult with me about a strategy once I get the basic information we will need to begin our search."

The woman frowned. "I see. How old are you?"

"Old enough," I assured her. Being a small woman, barely five feet in height, often led people to believe I was younger than I actually am. I pulled out a notepad and pen. "Is there somewhere you would like to sit while we chat?"

"How about out on the lanai? It is a beautiful day today. Not at all as hot as it has been."

I had to agree with that. It was a beautiful day. "So I have your husband's name, age, and occupation, but I'd like to go over everything again to make sure there are no errors."

"Okay."

I read my notes which told me that Kinsley Palakiko was a sixty-eight-year-old retired airline pilot who was last seen on Saturday around lunchtime when he left his home to do errands. He never came home. Hoku called and spoke to my father yesterday when her husband still had not called or shown up. He'd completed a basic questionnaire over the phone. He'd traced the man's phone, tracked his credit cards, and conducted a GPS search for his car. It was determined that the phone had been turned off, the GPS on the car was disabled, and the credit cards had not been used. We did live on an island, and the man was a retired airline pilot, so Dad checked with the airlines that served the island, but none reported activity from Kinsley in over a month. Hoku verified that the two of them had gone to the mainland for a week just about a month ago and that neither of them had traveled from the island since.

"If your husband felt the need to get away and didn't want to be found for whatever reason, where would he go?" I asked.

"You think my husband is off having some sort of a fling?"

"Not necessarily," I answered. "However, statistically speaking, more missing persons turn out not to have been the victim of foul play than turn out to have been. It is smart to look at all options."

"So you think Kinsley is just fine. You think he has put me through what is by far the worst few days of my life for nothing."

"Again, I'm not necessarily saying that." I paused and looked at the woman who seemed to be more angry than scared and I found myself wondering if she wasn't being overly dramatic for my benefit. "When your husband didn't come home after two days, why did you call Pope Investigations? Why didn't you call the police?"

The woman lowered her gaze but didn't respond right away.

"You don't think he has met with foul play either. You think he simply took off and you want him found. You may even believe that he is missing because he is engaged in some sort of illegal activity and you didn't want to get the authorities involved."

"That's a lot of speculation," the woman accused.

"Perhaps. But I'm not wrong, am I?"

"Kinsley likes to gamble. He isn't very good at it and has lost most of our retirement savings over the past couple of years. He'd been out late on Friday, and we didn't speak, but when he came to bed, I could smell the smoke and alcohol that accompany a backroom poker game, so I knew. He left around lunchtime on Saturday, simply saying that he had errands he needed to do. He didn't elaborate or say when he'd be home, but I assumed he'd be home in a few hours. When he didn't come home at all that day, I assumed his errands had led to a Saturday night poker game. I tried calling him about a million times, but the calls went straight to voicemail. I waited until Monday, hoping he would show up, but when he didn't, I decided to call your father. Kinsley has gone off on gambling binges in the past, but this time feels different.

"Different how?"

"For one thing, he has been away longer than usual."

I made a few notes and then looked up at the woman. "So if your husband is just off gambling somewhere, which it sounds like he very well may be, why did you think we would be able to find him when you couldn't?"

"Finding people is your job. I figured you'd have a few tricks that I didn't know to try."

I supposed we did have a few tricks that the missing man's wife didn't know to try, but now that I suspected he had taken off on his own free will, I wasn't sure I wanted to get in the middle of a marital spat. Still, there was a slim possibility that the man really had met with foul play. And I asked the woman several more questions, mostly relating to her husband's friends, lodging preferences, and financial situation. I promised to do what I could and to call her with an update by the following morning. I also took down the information relating to his car. It wouldn't hurt to ask my brothers and friends with HPD to keep an eye out for it. As I drove back to Pope

Investigations, I made a mental list of people to talk to. If the man was a gambler, I was sure my friend, Emmy Jean Thornton, would know the guy. On the surface, Emmy Jean was a sassy southern sex kitten, but beneath the Dolly Parton exterior, was a shrewd woman who could out drink and out gamble most of the men on the island.

Chapter 2

After my meeting with Hoku, I returned to Pope Investigations. Dad's car was in the drive, and additional HPD vehicles had shown up. I parked off to the side of the building and then headed toward the front door where the crime scene guys were working to collect physical evidence. The front door had been wrapped with yellow crime scene tape, so I asked the man closest to me if he knew where Jason might be. When he told me that he was in the office in the back of the building speaking to my father, I decided to head around to the rear of the building to access the office through the back door so as to avoid the men who were working in the lobby.

"Oh, good, you're back," Dad said as I entered the office from the hallway. "How did things go with Mrs. Palakiko?"

"The interview went fine. There are some things we can check out, but I suspect the guy is just off on a gambling spree." I looked at Jason. "So what do we know about the victim I found laid out across the entry this morning?"

"According to the driver's license found in the victim's pocket, his name is Ano Hanale. He is a twenty-eight-year-old resident of Oahu living right here on the North Shore. One of the guys from the crime scene unit recognized the man as owning a food truck in the area. At this point, I'm waiting for additional information."

"So our victims so far are a twenty-eight-year-old food truck owner, a forty-six-year-old nightclub owner, and a sixty-eight-year-old retired Air Force officer vacationing in the area. What on earth do these three men have in common, and, maybe even more importantly, what do they have to do with me?"

"That is the question of the hour," Dad said.

I leaned a hip against Dad's desk. "It seems unlikely that the men knew each other. The first victim resided in San Diego, California, and had only been on the island for a short time when he was found dead. The second victim lived and worked in Honolulu, and it sounds like the third victim lived and worked on the North Shore. There is a forty year age difference between the oldest and youngest victim, and the occupations of each man are about as different as one can get."

"Maybe they didn't know each other, but they still could have had something in common," Jason pointed out. "They could all have received rides from the same Uber driver, or they could have all eaten at the same restaurant. If we look hard enough, I suspect we'll find a link between the three of them and you." Jason paused. The expression on his face indicated that he was working the situation through in his mind.

"Maybe the link is the resort where you work. I'll check to see if the first victim stayed there at some point. At the time of his death, he'd been renting a condo, but that doesn't mean he didn't stay at the resort prior to that." Jason paused and furrowed his brow. "I doubt the nightclub owner was staying at the resort, but he could have been on the premises to promote his club. And the most recent victim, the food truck guy, I suppose he could have just been in the area to surf."

"It seems like a stretch, but I'll play along," I said. "There are a lot of people in and out of the Dolphin Bay Resort for a variety of reasons, and not just the hotel guests. We have several restaurants, a couple of bars, and a public beach with decent surfing." I crossed the room and sat down on one of the chairs provided for just that purpose. "The thing is, there are so many people in and out of there, how will we ever narrow it down even if the resort, or a portion of the resort, is the link?"

"I don't know," Jason admitted.

"And if the resort is the link, how did the killer know where Lani lives?" Dad asked. "The first victim was found on the beach behind the condo."

"That's true." Jason drummed his fingers on the desk in front of him. He looked at me. "Are you sure you don't recognize any of the three men?"

"The last victim, the food truck guy. I thought I recognized him when I stumbled upon his body this morning. Now that I know he runs a food truck, I'm pretty sure I remember seeing him parked just down the beach from the resort where Dolphin Bay Beach gives way to the public park. He sells fish tacos, shrimp sandwiches, and other offerings from the sea."

"So it is possible, even likely, that a guest staying at the resort could have walked down the beach and bought lunch from Mr. Hanale?"

"Sure."

"Do we know when the first victim, Walter Evans, arrived on the island?" Dad asked. "His body was found on the beach behind Lani's condo twenty days ago. I'm curious if he had just arrived or if he had been here for a while."

"Mr. Evans did not arrive via commercial air," Jason answered. "I was able to determine that at the time of his death, he was staying in a condo about a half mile east of Lani's place. He'd rented the condo six days prior to his death, and he had plans to stay another week. Since I don't know how he arrived on the island, I was never able to determine when he arrived. It could be that his arrival coincided with his stay at the condo, but it is also possible that he arrived prior to that and stayed somewhere else."

"Did you check cruise ships?" Dad asked.

"I did, but that didn't pan out," Jason confirmed. "At this point, I am going to assume that Mr. Evans arrived on the island via private boat, helicopter, or airplane."

"What about his credit cards?" I asked.

"The only credit card I could find in his name was last used two months prior to his death in a coffee shop in San Francisco, California. The condo where he'd been staying when he died had been paid for ahead of time, and if he ate out or rented a car, he must have used cash or perhaps possessed an additional credit card we have not discovered yet."

"Does this whole thing sound just a tad too covert operations to you?" I asked.

"Actually, it does," Jason agreed. "Not only could I not find a recent paper trail, but the man was not found with a phone on his person, and I was unable to find a cell registered to him. If I had to guess, the guy was on the island to hide out and intentionally behaved in such a way so as not to be found.'

"Hide out from who?" I asked.

Jason shrugged. "No idea."

"Was Mr. Evans married?" Dad asked.

"No. He never married nor had children. He never held a job other than the Air Force from which he retired ten years ago. Since his retirement, it appears he has traveled extensively. His passport shows trips to Europe, South America, the Middle East, and most recently, Japan."

Dad got up, walked over to the window, and looked out to the sea. His eyes narrowed a little before he turned from the window and looked at Jason. "Okay, so this guy is well traveled. It appears he arrived on Oahu by means other than commercial transportation, and it looks as if he behaved in such a manner as not to leave a trail of any sort. It sounds like the actions of a man involved in criminal activity."

"I don't disagree," Jason said, "but the guy has an impressive resume with the Air Force leading right up until his retirement. When I read over his list of accomplishments, he didn't strike me as being the sort of person to be up to something sinister."

"People change," Dad said.

"I suppose they do," Jason agreed.

"So what about the second victim?" I asked. "The nightclub owner. Any suspicious activity on his part?"

"Not really," Jason said. "Vinnie Travano owned a nightclub in Honolulu. He had a clean record and, based on interviews conducted after his death ten days ago, he was well liked by his employees, neighbors, and even his competitors. As you know, he was found propped up on Lani's lifeguard tower at the Dolphin Bay Resort. Prior to that, he was last seen at his nightclub two days prior."

"He was found on Saturday," I said. "If he was last seen on Thursday, was he supposed to show up at the nightclub on Friday?"

"According to his manager, when he left in the wee hours of the morning on Thursday, he told his staff that he needed to take care of a personal matter and might be out for a few days. No one we spoke to knew what that personal matter might have pertained to."

"What about phone and credit card records?" Dad asked.

"The last charge he made was at a gas station in Honolulu shortly after he left the club on Thursday. I spoke to Mr. Travano's neighbors in an attempt to determine the last time anyone saw him at home, but Mr. Travano lives in a high rise, and the neighbors don't really pay that much attention to the comings and goings of their neighbors. I didn't find evidence that our victim rented a lodging property, so it is possible that he was not staying on the North Shore. Of course, he could have been staying with a friend who hasn't come forward."

"So we have a retired Air Force officer who arrived on the island in an unknown manner and was here for an unknown purpose, and a nightclub owner who took some time off to see to a personal matter," I said. "And then there is today's victim, the food truck owner. Do we know anything about his movements during the past few days?"

"Not yet, but I'll let you know if I find anything. At this point, I'm not even a hundred percent certain the deaths are linked. I realize that they appear to be, but while all three victims were shot, the weapons used to kill them appear to be three different guns." Jason looked up as his partner stuck his head in the door to let him know that Ano Hanale's roommate was on the phone. Jason answered the call, and Dad and I took our cue and headed out onto the lanai at the back of the building.

"So what do you think?" I asked Dad.

"I think that a world traveler who showed up on the island under the radar and a nightclub owner could be involved in the same shady dealings, perhaps involving smuggling, money laundering, or even drugs, but if that is the case, I have no idea how a food truck owner and my daughter fit into the whole thing. We need more information."

"Agreed. We can do some digging, but first, we should talk about our missing husband. Our client is paying us a lot of money to track him down."

Dad sat down on an outdoor swing. "Okay. What do we know?"

I went over my notes from this afternoon, taking my time and sharing my overall impressions of the client as well as the details she provided. It did seem as if the guy might have simply taken off, but Dad suggested that we talk to his friends and business associates before jumping to any conclusions. I agreed, so we made up a list of people to start with. We divided the list between us, and each set off in different directions after letting Jason know what we were doing and obtaining his promise to bring us into the loop if he came up with new information relating to the murder cases.

Chapter 3

I decided to start my investigation with a chat with Emmy Jean Thornton, a woman I'd met while accompanying my neighbor to bingo at the senior center. I'd called her earlier, and she'd informed me that she was having a spa day with her sister, Tammy Rhea, but that I was welcome to pop in during their tanning hour by the pool if I wanted to chat. Normally the spa did not allow individuals who were not paying customers into the spa and pool area, but the manager on duty today used to work at the Dolphin Bay Resort, so I'd called ahead and asked her to leave me a pass at the desk.

"Lani darling," greeted Emmy Jean with her big hair piled high on her head, and her even bigger breasts spilling out of a tiny aqua blue bikini top. I had to hand it to her, the sequined swimsuit was not one that could be pulled off by most sixty-four-year-olds, but somehow she managed to make it work.

"Emmy Jean, Tammy Rhea," I greeted the sisters. "It's been a while."

"Far too long in my opinion," Tammy Rhea responded. "In fact, I don't think you've been to a single bingo game since going into business with your father."

"I've been a lot busier since we opened Pope Investigations," I admitted. "I do miss those Monday lunches, however. I'll try to free up some time in the next few weeks."

"Everyone would love to see you, although we've moved the lunches to Wednesdays."

"Good to know."

"You said you had questions relating to Kinsley Palakiko," Emmy Jean stated.

I nodded. "His wife hired us to find him. I guess he has been missing since Saturday. I understand that the man has a gambling problem, and figured that the two of you might have crossed paths."

"You figured correctly," Emmy Jean said. She picked up a glass that looked to be filled with flavored vodka of some sort and took a sip. "Kinsley is a regular at my Friday night poker game, and I know he frequents other games as well. To be honest, the man is one of the worst poker players I've ever come across. Not only does he lose the majority of the time, but he also loses big. If I had to guess, if he is missing, he most likely blew through his savings and ended up in debt to the wrong person."

"And which wrong person might that be?"

Emmy Jean shrugged. "I really wouldn't know. There are a lot of money lenders out there that you don't want to end up owing money to."

"Was he in attendance at the poker game this past Friday?" I asked.

"He was."

"And did he lose?"

Emmy Jean frowned, creasing her perfectly sculpted brow. "Actually, he didn't. In fact, he won big, which believe me, was a first." Emmy Jean pursed her lips. "You know, you might want to talk to a man named Spade. He attended the Friday game, and I remember him inviting Kinsley to a private game at his estate on Saturday night. I don't know if he went, but the man was flush with cash after Friday's game, so chances are he did."

"Does Spade have a last name?" I asked. "Or even a real first name?"

Emmy Jean shook her head. "Nope, Spade is his only name as far as I know. If you want to have a conversation with the man, you should chat with McCarthy. I know he frequents the Saturday night games from time to time."

Mike McCarthy was a friend of my dad's, also a retired cop, who, along with the other two Stooges, Ben Woodson and Frank Thomas, helped us out with our investigations from time to time. Each of the three men had their strengths and their vices. McCarthy's vice just happened to be gambling.

"Okay. I'll call him. Is there anything else you can tell me about Kinsley that might help me track him down?"

"I know he is a pilot," Emmy Jean said. "It seems to me that he has a marketable trade that would earn him a lot of cash if he was able to hook up with someone wanting to come and go from the island undetected. I'm not making any sort of an official statement, but the word on the street is that there is a player on the island who brokers that sort of thing. From what I heard, the broker is a woman known in certain circles for being able to provide transportation for anyone needing to get on or off the island under the radar. That is if you have enough cash."

"Do you know the name of this woman?"

Emmy Jean lifted a tanned shoulder. "Unfortunately, I am not privy to any specific information. You know that I don't like to get involved in those sorts of things. However, not wanting to get involved doesn't mean I don't hear things. In this case, what I've heard are generalized statements lacking any real details."

After I'd gotten everything out of Emmy Jean I felt I was going to get out of her, I said my goodbyes and returned to my car. I called McCarthy, but he didn't answer, so I left a voicemail asking him to call me. Then I called my dad with the information that Kinsley might have a side job flying people in and out of the islands under the radar. He said he'd look into it, so I headed home.

After I arrived home, I greeted my dog, Sandy, and then headed toward my bedroom to change into my swimsuit. It was much too beautiful of an afternoon to spend it indoors. The waves were pretty unspectacular today, but an unspectacular day on the water was still better than a spectacular day on land. I glanced at Kekoa's bedroom door. It was closed, and I hadn't heard her moving around, so I wondered if she was napping. Her car was in the drive, so I knew she hadn't gone anywhere, and I knew she hadn't been sleeping well since her boyfriend, Cameron Carrington, had moved from the island after being offered a job as a Los Angeles County lifeguard, a position that he had dreamed of for most of his adult life. When the job offer came through, I'd been happy for Cam, but sad for Kekoa. I knew from experience that saying goodbye to the man you love is one of the hardest things one can do.

My relationship with my boyfriend, Luke Austin, had been very much up in the air since the previous October when his father, who owned a huge cattle ranch in Texas, had been injured in an accident. Luke had flown home to help out while his dad was in the hospital. He'd planned to be back as soon as his father was healed enough to take over the management of the ranch, but just when it seemed the end was in sight, Luke's father suffered a fatal heart attack, and Luke extended his stay indefinitely.

Luke and I had been trying to hold our relationship together, but I had to admit it was getting harder and harder to do so. Luke's dad passed away in November, so he'd been forced to cancel his trip to the island for Thanksgiving. I'd gone to Texas for two weeks at Christmas, but while I'd been happy to spend time with Luke, I'd missed my family and the life I'd built here on the island. In January, Cam had announced that he was moving to LA, and I'd made the decision to move from Luke's place, where I was pretty miserable living by myself, back into the apartment I had shared with Kekoa and Cam before to moving into Luke's place just prior to his father's passing. I'd hoped Luke would find his way back to me, but in February, he asked Brody Waller, the friend who was housesitting his property, to accompany his dogs, Duke and Dallas, to Texas. In my heart, I knew that the dogs leaving the island most likely signaled the end, but I hadn't been ready to throw in the towel, and Luke swore he wasn't ready to end things either.

In April, Luke asked Brody to sell off the last of his livestock. Brody still lived in the house Luke owned, and Luke still made noises about coming home as soon as things settled down, but in my heart, I knew he wouldn't. In those moments when I had the clarity to step back and look at things objectively, I think I always knew that our happily ever after was never going to be.

Technically, we were still a couple. The calls between us had become less frequent, but we did try to connect at least once a week. The long calls filled with angst and longing we'd once shared had melded into short conversations about local events. The fact that Luke hadn't sold his house yet, left me clinging to a thread of hope that he actually would return one day, but the fact that I could feel him pulling away seemed to indicate that he wouldn't. In the eight months Luke had been away, we really hadn't talked about the future in terms of our relationship, but I supposed that perhaps it was time we did.

As I walked past the other five apartments toward the beach, I thought about each neighbor. Kekoa and I lived in unit one, and Elva Talbot lived in apartment two. She was decades older than Kekoa and me, but we depended on her more than any of the others. In many ways, she was like a second mother to us. She had been the one to hold me as I shed the zillion tears I'd needed to shed to get on with my life once I realized Luke wasn't coming back any time soon.

Apartment three was currently empty. The tenants who had lived there moved to the mainland two months ago, and for some reason, the owner of the building hadn't leased out the unit to new tenants yet. Carina West lived in apartment four, but she had just become engaged, so I suspected she'd be moving out soon as well. Apartment five belonged to our good friends, Kevin Green and Sean Trainor, flight attendants who were away as much as they were home, and apartment number six belonged to a man I knew only as Shredder. I knew that Shredder was some sort of top-secret spy who worked for an unnamed organization which seemed to have a wide reach and a lot of power. He came and went often, but when he'd taken off nine months ago, he had never returned. At times, I wondered if he was dead, but he still paid his rent, so I supposed that he must be still alive somewhere in the world.

I unzipped my sweatshirt and was about to toss it down on my towel when I heard my phone ding. I noticed that I had a missed call from Luke. When we'd last spoken, he'd agreed to consider a trip to Oahu at the end of the month, but needed to check on some things first. I really hoped he'd come. This long distance thing was really not working, and I felt the need to speak to him in person about where, if anywhere, we went from here.

I found a place to sit in the sun and then hit the call back button. It went to voicemail. "Hey, Luke. Sorry I missed your call. I've been busy all day, and what a day it's been. When I arrived at work this morning, I found a dead man lying across the entry just inside the front door. As you know, this makes my third body in twenty days. Jason is working on it, but Dad and I will probably jump in as well. I guess this is sort of a long message. Anyway, I hope everything is going to work out for you to come for a visit this month. I miss you." I hung up without adding the usual *I love you*. I wasn't sure what that was all about because I did love Luke. I really did. Maybe I was pulling away emotionally the way I sensed that he'd been pulling away from me. Maybe we were both just trying to find a way to deal with what seemed to be an impossible situation.

I grabbed my surfboard and was about to head into the water when I saw Kekoa heading toward me. Deciding to wait, I set the surfboard down. I turned slightly so I could look more directly at my cousin. "I'm sensing that you had another rough night. Cam?"

Kekoa turned her head and looked at me. "Actually, no. Don't get me wrong, I still miss Cam, more than I can say, but my funk this afternoon has more to do with the fact that my boss decided to give the promotion I deserved and was led to believe I would receive, to the new girl that started just a month ago."

"Oh, Kekoa, I'm so sorry. I can't believe he did that. You totally deserved the promotion. What was the dude thinking?"

"I think that he was thinking that he might have a shot of sleeping with Lisa; whereas, I made it clear that I was not interested in sleeping my way to the top." Kekoa blew out a breath. "I know you have been telling me to quit for months, and I have resisted the suggestion, but I'm done. If the management of the Dolphin Bay Resort doesn't value my contribution, they can find someone else willing to work so many hours of overtime."

I placed my hand on Kekoa's arm. "I'm sorry about the promotion, but I'm not sorry you are finally ready to quit. I don't suppose you have reconsidered working full-time for Dad and me."

Kekoa frowned. "Actually, I might be willing to talk about expanding my hours. Now that you are getting clients on a steady basis, you really do need someone in the office to answer phones while you and Uncle Keanu are out investigating."

I hugged Kekoa. "Great. I think this is going to work out for all of us."

Kekoa hugged me back just a bit harder than normal. I pulled back and looked her in the eyes. "So is there something else you want to talk about?"

She shrugged. "You asked about Cam. I guess he is part of my down in the dumps mood. He called me last night so we could talk about the future of our relationship. When he first left, we pretty much decided to try the long distance thing, but after some time apart, I've come to the conclusion that there isn't a point in trying to retain any sort of relationship other than a friendship. He loves his new job. He shared that he really has no plans to move back to Hawaii, and I just can't see myself moving to LA." Kekoa took a shaky breath. "I used to think that I would follow the right guy anywhere. I suppose my unwillingness to move to LA either means that I was wrong or that Cam isn't the right guy."

"I'm sorry. I know how hard this is."

Kekoa smiled a sad little smile. "I know you do. And I'll be fine. I think that Cam and I just need to pull the Band-Aid off and realize that we don't have a future together. I think we need to accept that there will be a period of pain that must be endured before we can move on, but eventually, we will work through our grief and will be better off for it. It just makes zero sense to hang onto something that is just not meant to be."

Chapter 4

Wednesday, June 26

It had been three weeks since I'd found Walter Evans' body lying on the beach behind the condo where I lived. He'd been shot once through the chest, although no one had seen or heard a thing. The body was wet, so initially, Jason suspected that the man had been dumped at sea and had coincidentally washed up at the beach behind the condo. And this could still turn out to be the case, but now that I had found three victims in twenty days, it seemed more likely that the body had been placed there.

The man had been dressed casually in a pair of Khaki pants and a colorful Hawaiian shirt. He'd been a large man. Before his death, he'd stood six feet six inches tall, and it seemed apparent that he'd continued his fitness routine even after retiring from the service. If a single man had carried Walter from the road to the beach, he would have had to have been a large man himself, so the odds were there were at least two individuals involved, or the body had been deposited on the beach from a boat.

Dad and I talked about the fact that the extensive traveling the man did before being shot could very well indicate activity other than simply tourism. Like our missing person, Walter had been a pilot, so I had to wonder if he made extra cash by transporting individuals who wanted to travel under the radar. Of course, it also occurred to me that the man might be involved in some sort of spy game, or, perhaps the sale of illegal contraband, or given the fact that he had been in the military, even the sale of sensitive information. Really, at this point, the sky seemed to be the limit in terms of a possible motive, until you factored in the fact that the body of the victim seemed to have been left for me to find and that two other bodies had likewise been left at places I was known to frequent. When you took that into account, the number of motives for any of the deaths seemed to decrease significantly.

"It looks like the guys are home," I said to Sandy, as we walked from the beach toward our condo. Sean Trainor and Kevin Green were both flight attendants, who not only traveled extensively for work but traveled extensively for pleasure as well. They'd been away for almost a month, so I was happy to see they were back. As I passed the front window of their condo, I glanced inside to find Sean standing at the kitchen counter, drinking a cup of coffee. I waved to him, and he waved me in.

"Welcome back," I said.

"It's good to be back." Sean handed me a cup of coffee and then offered a dog biscuit to Sandy. "Kevin and I had a wonderful time in the Caribbean, but four weeks is too long to stay in one general area. I'm actually looking forward to going back to work next week."

"Are you still doing the Honolulu to Las Vegas flight?"

"Actually, I'm going to be working the flight to Paris for a few months. I'm looking forward to the change of pace." Sean topped off his coffee. "Listen, if you aren't busy, Kevin and I want to have the gang over for enchiladas and margaritas tonight."

"You want to do it tonight? You just got home. Aren't you exhausted?"

"Not a bit," Sean waved a hand.

"I'm free. I'll ask Kekoa, but I don't think she has plans."

"Fabulous. I asked Elva, and she's in, and I was going to pop by and chat with Carina after she wakes up. It looks like unit three is still empty."

"So far, it is. I know the owner wanted to paint the place and put new tile in the entry, so that may be what is holding things up."

"Still no word from Shredder?"

I frowned as the image of the tenant from unit six flashed through my mind. "No. And I have to admit that I'm getting worried. I know he has a tendency to disappear without telling anyone, but it's been months. Where on earth could he be for so long?"

"His stuff is still here, so it looks like he is paying his rent. I'm sure he's fine. Knowing Shredder, he's just been chasing the waves wherever they've taken him. He'll be back. Eventually."

I chatted with Sean for a few more minutes and then headed toward my apartment to shower and change for work. I was curious as to what my dad might have found out about any of our three murder victims or our missing person. I'd chatted with him yesterday afternoon, but at the time of our conversation, he'd still had several leads to track down.

"Sean and Kevin are back," I said to Kekoa when she walked out of her bedroom, and into the kitchen. "They're doing enchiladas and margaritas tonight."

"That sounds like exactly the sort of thing I need. What time?"

"Seven. I figure we should be home from work by six unless we turn up a hot lead on one of the cases we are working on."

"Jason called while you were out with Sandy. He was leaving his house and heading into the office, so he said he'd just call you later this morning."

"Did he say what he wanted?"

"No. Just that he needed to ask you about something and would call you later."

I topped off my coffee. "Okay. I'm going to jump in the shower. We can ride to the office together if you want."

"Sounds fine. I'm going to make a sandwich to bring for lunch. If I am going to exist on only one job now, I'm going to need to learn to budget."

Kekoa was one of the most financially responsible people I knew. She made a good salary at the resort, and she worked for Pope Investigation part-time as well, so I supposed that quitting the resort and working full-time for Dad and me would result in a drop in income, but neither of us was really extravagant, so I was sure it would all work out fine.

After stripping off my sandy clothes, I stepped into the cool spray of the shower. As I washed my hair, I realized that I had never hooked up with Luke yesterday. Sometimes I wondered why we continued to try when the situation really was hopeless. Luke had responsibilities in Texas, and no matter how hard I tried, I simply could not imagine myself living there. Kekoa had made a comment about following the right guy anywhere, and since she'd been unwilling to follow Cam to LA, that must mean he wasn't the right guy. She'd made a really good point, which the more I thought about it, really did seem to apply to Luke and me as well.

Kekoa was ready to head out by the time I got out of the bathroom, so I slipped on a pair of capris and a cool top given the heat of the day. I slipped on a pair of sandals, grabbed Sandy's leash, and headed out to the parking area. Kekoa and I talked about the three men I'd found dead in the past three weeks as we made the drive from our condo to the office, and we both agreed that figuring how I fit into the equation was going to be the key.

Kekoa got to work making the coffee and retrieving the messages from the machine while I headed directly into Dad's office.

"Morning," I said, sitting down across from him.

"Walter Evans didn't stay at the Dolphin Bay Resort, but he did meet a woman there on several occasions," Dad jumped right in. "The woman checked in under the name Samantha Jones, but it looks like that is a fake name. I have Jason running her photo through the facial recognition software he has access to. Chances are she is in the system."

"Okay, so victim number one has a link to the resort where I work one day a week and victim number three sells food out of his truck just down the beach. What about our nightclub owner? I know his body was left at the resort for me to find, but is there evidence he had spent time there prior to his death?"

"I haven't found any evidence that he spent time at the resort yet, but I'll keep looking. The main question in my mind at this point, is even if we can place Vinnie Travano at the resort in the time period leading up to his death, what does that mean? Why would being at or near the resort lead to becoming a victim?"

"Maybe someone who either works at or is staying at the resort is our killer," I suggested.

"Even if that were true, why these three men? And even if we could find the link between the three men, why were all three victims left in locations where you would be the one to find them?"

All good questions for which I didn't have an answer. "What if the three men are all part of the same operation? Maybe our well-traveled pilot is transporting some illegal product, and the nightclub owner is laundering the money. I'm not sure where the food truck guy comes in. Maybe he is involved in distribution. Buy a taco for ten grand and get a free firearm, or whatever it is they are dealing."

"Sounds like a stretch, and even if that were true, who did the killing and, again, the question of the hour, why leave the bodies for you to find? I guess at this point, we'll just keep digging. I am motivated to find the woman Evans met with. I thought I'd take her photo down to the area where Hanale's food truck had been parked, and see if any of the regulars remember seeing her. Do you want to come along? We can grab an early lunch while we're there."

"Sounds good to me. I'm starving."

We arrived at the public park to find the truck Hanale had owned open for business. It seemed that our victim was partners with his cousin, Keo, who'd decided to keep the truck open in spite of his recent loss. According to Keo, he'd seen the woman in the photo on several occasions. Dad asked him when he had first noticed the woman, and Keo answered that he thought it was about three to four weeks ago. That loosely fit the timeline we'd established for Walter Evans' visit to the island.

"How about this guy," Dad showed Keo a photo of Evans. "Do you remember seeing him?"

"Yeah. I saw him talking to Ano a while back. Maybe a month ago. Maybe less. I can't really be sure."

"Do you know what they were talking about?" Dad asked.

"No. Ano walked away to have his discussion. I asked Ano about it, and he just said the guy wanted him to cater an event. We do events all the time, so I really didn't give it a second thought."

"Do you remember seeing the man in the area on any other occasion?' I asked.

"No, just the one time," Keo answered.

"What about this man?" Dad held up a photo of the nightclub owner.

Keo took the photo and looked at it closely. "I don't remember seeing the guy here, but I know who he is. His name is Vinnie. I know he owns a nightclub on the South Shore. And I know he is friends with a guy I know named Spade."

"You are friends with Spade?" Dad asked.

The man shrugged. "The word friend is a generous term. Let's just say that we have had occasion to do business together in the past."

"Business?" Dad asked.

"Let's just say that Spade and I share a common interest." Keo turned around and looked back toward the truck. "I need to get back. Ano was a good guy. I hope you figure out who did this to him."

After Keo walked away, I glanced at my father. "That is the second time Spade has come up. First, in relation to our missing person, and now in relation to our third victim."

"It seems like it might be worth our while to track him down. You said your friend knows Spade. Do you think she knows where we can find him?"

"I don't think so. Emmy Jean didn't even know his real name." I paused to think about it. "She mentioned that Kinsley Palakiko attended her Friday night poker game, and she also mentioned that after the poker game, Spade invited him to a game the following night at his private estate. I suppose it might not hurt to question the others who attended the Friday night game. There could be someone in the group who attended the Saturday night game. I'll call Emmy Jean, and see if she knows where the Saturday night games are held and if she can give me any names, and you might want to call McCarthy. Emmy Jean made a comment about him attending the Saturday night games. I meant to mention it to you yesterday, but then I got distracted with the murder investigation."

"There's a table in the shade over near the little park. Let's head over there and make our calls."

A brief discussion with Emmy Jean netted me the information that the Saturday night games were for men only, so she had never been invited to attend, a situation which she was not at all happy with. She reminded me that McCarthy had been to the game, and suggested I talk to him. I let her know my dad was speaking to him but wondered if she knew of anyone else who might have information that could help us track down Kinsley Palakiko. She told me that she'd text me the names and contact information for a few others who attended the Friday night game if Dad's conversation with McCarthy didn't provide us with the information we needed.

"McCarthy wants to meet for lunch," Dad informed me after I'd hung up with Emmy Jean.

"I guess it's a good thing we haven't eaten yet. Where does he want to meet?"

"Callahan's. Thomas and Woodson will be there as well."

Callahan's was a bar that, while technically open to the public, was generally the type of establishment where men in blue and their guests could meet in a relaxed atmosphere. They also served decent food. Since I'd been working with Dad, we'd gone there for lunch fairly often. Thomas, Woodson, and McCarthy were retired cops who liked to hang out at Callahan's and talk about the good old days on the force. My dad used to hang out with them on almost a daily basis, but now that we'd opened the detective agency, he had much less time to hang out and shoot the breeze. Still, Dad knew his friends were a valuable resource, so he stayed in touch and would often ask for their opinion about a case we were working on.

"So what do you want to know?" McCarthy asked after Dad and I had met the three men in the bar.

Dad explained about our missing person, as well as our three murder victims. He informed the men that a man who went by the name of Spade had come up on more than one occasion, and he was interested in speaking to him.

"Spade won't talk to just anyone," McCarthy informed Dad. "And he definitely won't speak to a cop. But you are retired the same as me, so he might be willing to participate in an interview with the right incentive."

"What sort of incentive?" Dad asked.

McCarthy shrugged. "Don't know. I guess it boils down to whether or not you have something he might need."

"I take it you have his address?" Dad asked.

"I do, but it won't do you any good to show up without an appointment. The guy lives in a fortress. Between his security staff and his security system, no one gets in without an invitation."

"Can you help us with that?" I asked.

McCarthy creased his brow as if considering the question.

"What about approaching Spade through the new wife," Woodson suggested. "Spade tends to go through wives as often as I go through gym socks, but I know he recently married a woman named Jasmine Baine, and if I remember correctly, Jasmine and Luke are friends."

"Jasmine used to board her horse at Luke's," I confirmed. "We've chatted on several occasions. I'm sure Brody has her number. I'll call her, and see if she is willing to set up an appointment between her husband and us."

Luckily, a call to Brody netted me Jasmine's number. I called and explained the situation. She was hesitant to get in the middle her husband's business dealings and wasn't comfortable making an appointment with him on our behalf. She was willing to share the information that her husband was currently at home but would be going out in about an hour to meet up with a friend. Deciding that was the only real lead I had at this point, I decided to stakeout the house, wait for Spade to leave, and then follow him.

Chapter 5

One of the things I really hadn't anticipated about becoming a private investigator was the amount of time I would spend sitting around waiting for someone to show up or waiting for something to happen. Don't get me wrong, I knew that good old fashion stakeouts were part of the job description, but what I didn't know was what a large percentage of my time would be spent looking for a clue, rather than following up on that clue once discovered.

I glanced at the clock. I'd only been sitting in front of Spade's estate for sixty minutes, but it seemed longer. Much, much, longer. Maybe I should have filled my dad in on my plan. He would have insisted on coming along, which really wasn't necessary, but at least I would have had someone to talk to and wouldn't be quite so bored. Of course, Dad mentioned that he had his own clue to follow up on, so chances were he wouldn't have been able to join me anyway.

At the time I spoke to Jasmine, she'd said that her husband was going to be leaving in an hour. At this point, it had been almost ninety minutes since our conversation. Maybe he'd changed his mind. Maybe she'd been lying just to get me off the phone. I'd suspect that Spade may have left via a road at the back of the place, but the estate was bordered on three sides by the sea, so the entrance I was watching would be the only road in to or out of the property.

Deciding to take a closer look, I got out of my car and approached the entrance gate. A native Hawaiian wearing Khakis, with a gun strapped to his belt, manned it. I knew it would be useless to simply walk up to the estate and ask to speak to Spade, so I followed the wall around until it met the sea. I then turned and headed back in the other direction until I once again ran into the sea. At least I'd confirmed my suspicion that the only way in or out of the estate was through the gate unless, of course, you came by boat.

I headed back to my car and slipped into the driver's seat. I was debating whether to wait a while longer or give up and head home when my passenger door opened. I gasped and then smiled when a man wearing board shorts and a tank top slipped onto the passenger side seat. "Shredder." I leaned forward and hugged the man. "What are you doing here?"

Shredder hugged me back. "I was about to ask you the same thing."

"I'm waiting for a man named Spade to leave the estate so I can follow him. I think he might be connected to a missing person we've been hired to find. Where have you been all this time?"

Shredder shrugged. "Around. What do you mean that you've been hired to find a missing person?"

"Dad and I opened a PI agency. A woman named Hokulani Palakiko hired us to find her husband, Kinsley, after he failed to come home after two days. He hasn't been seen since Saturday morning. Are you back? I mean really back? To stay?"

Shredder narrowed his gaze. "Why do you think Spade is connected to this missing person you are looking for?"

As usual, Shredder only answered the questions he wanted to answer and ignored the rest.

"Kinsley Palakiko likes to gamble. According to Emmy Jean, who also likes to gamble, he frequently attends the same Friday night game she does. This past Friday, he was in attendance and won big. Emmy Jean told me that Spade was there, and invited him to his private Saturday night game. He's been missing ever since, so I thought Spade might have information that would help us track the guy down."

"Are you sure he even showed up to the game on Saturday?"

I stared at Shredder before answering. I still couldn't believe he was sitting in the passenger seat of my Jeep as if the past nine months had never happened. He'd lost his golden tan. In fact, he was downright pale. I had to assume he'd been somewhere cold during his time away. Or at least somewhere that didn't allow him to spend his days in the sun as he had when he was here.

"Lani?"

"I'm not sure, actually. Emmy Jean told me that Kinsley had been invited to the game. I really have no way of knowing if he went. I sort of hoped Spade could fill in a few blanks if I can ever manage to get in front of the guy."

"And your plan to do that is to sit here until he comes out and then what? Accost the man?"

I rolled my eyes. "Of course not. I spoke to his new wife who happens to be a friend of Luke's, and she told me that he planned to leave the estate for a meeting about an hour from the time we spoke. My plan had been to follow him and try to figure it out from there. It's been more than an hour though so he must have changed his mind or Jasmine might have been mistaken."

"So I guess you and Luke must be married by now."

I was surprised by the abrupt change in the subject but decided to answer. "No. We aren't married. Luke is in Texas. He has been in Texas since October. To be honest, I sort of doubt he will ever come back."

Shredder's face softened. "So you are no longer a couple?"

"I don't know. I guess technically, we are still a couple. It's complicated. Can we get back to the reason you are here?"

Shredder didn't answer right away.

"You were watching him too." I realized. I knew that Shredder was some sort of a spy who worked for the government or at least a government adjacent organization. "Is this Spade some sort of international criminal?"

"No, not really, but the guy tends to associate with dangerous men. Much too dangerous for you to be toying with. I want you to go home and forget you ever heard the name Spade."

"Like hell. It is beginning to sound like this guy is somehow part of whatever is going on with my missing person and possibly even the three bodies that have been left for me like some sort of sicko gift."

"Three bodies?"

I smiled. "You mean I know something the all-knowing Shredder doesn't know? You're slipping."

"I just arrived on the island a few hours ago. I was indisposed prior to that, so unable to stay on top of your comings and goings like I normally would. I can see that the timing of my incarceration was most unfortunate. So about the bodies?"

"Incarceration? Were you in prison?"

"Not a US prison. The bodies?"

I was about to fill him in when the exact words he used to explain his lack of knowledge of current affairs hit me. "Have you been watching me or tracking me or something?"

"I watch and track a lot of people. It's my job. Now back to the bodies. You said there were three? Who exactly has died, and what do you know about those deaths?"

I took a few minutes to fill Shredder in. I really didn't know a whole lot about any of the victims I'd stumbled across, but I shared what I knew. I even offered a few theories I was kicking around, which only made him frown even more deeply. It was during my expose of the roles of the men as a smuggler, a money launderer, and an illegal goods distributor that the gate to the estate opened. "That might be him." I put my hand on my key, which I'd left in the ignition.

Shredder put his hand over mine. "Wait."

"But we'll lose him."

"We won't lose him. Scrunch down a bit, so no one sees you."

I did as Shredder instructed.

A black four-door sedan with darkly tinted windows came through the gate. The man who was driving looked to be a paid driver, and there was no way to see who was in the backseat. As soon as the car committed to a direction, Shredder got out of my car and slipped around to the driver's side. "Scoot over."

"No way. This is my car. I'm driving."

"Not if you don't want to lose him. Now scoot over."

I did.

Shredder started my Jeep and then pulled onto the highway. He headed in the direction the sedan had taken. I was sure we'd lost him, but then I noticed the sedan make a turn just as we came over a small hill.

"There," I said. "He turned there."

"I saw him," Shredder sped up a bit, but not nearly enough in my opinion. If I had been the one driving, I would have stayed a lot closer, but Shredder seemed to maintain the furthest distance between the vehicles possible in which he was still able to see the car in front of him. If he made a quick turn or went into a parking garage, we'd lose him for sure.

"He's heading toward Kaena Point," I said.

"I bet he is headed to the Dillingham Airfield," Shredder slowed a bit as the car we were following slowed, probably due to the rough road.

"Do you think he is meeting someone or flying out?" I asked.

"I don't know. I guess we'll just watch and see what happens."

Shredder pulled the Jeep to a stop as we approached the airfield. The sedan seemed to be meeting a private jet that was already waiting. Two men got off the jet, and two men got out of the car to meet them.

"Are either of those men Spade?" I asked.

"The taller of the two men."

"I wish we could hear what they are saying." I squinted, but there was no way to read their lips from this distance, even if I could read lips, which I couldn't. "Do you recognize the men from the plane?"

"One of them. The man with him is most likely one of his goons. Do you recognize the man who is piloting the plane?"

I tried to focus in on the pilot who was barely visible through the windshield of the plane, but he was too far away. "I don't know. The plane is too far away for me to make out any details."

Shredder grabbed my hand. "Come on. Let's see if we can get closer."

Shredder led me toward a row of trees. They grew together closely in this area, so they provided good cover. We scooted along as quickly as we could, but at some point, we were going to have to venture out onto the tarmac if we wanted a good view of what was going on.

"I think if we make a run for it, we might be able to make it to those hangers without anyone seeing us. Stay low and make it fast."

"Okay," I said to Shredder. My heart was pounding at this point. I really didn't see any way that we'd make it to our destination without being spotted. Of course, the men were talking, which meant they were distracted, but what about the pilot who was still sitting in the cockpit? Surely, he'd notice us, even if the others didn't.

Once we arrived at the hangers, I paused to let my heart rate slow. Shredder scooted across the space until we were about as close to the plane as we were going to get. He motioned for me to take a close look at the pilot. I nodded.

"I think that is my missing person," I whispered. I held up my phone and snapped a photo using the zoom feature.

Shredder looked around the area as if trying to get an overview of the situation.

"It looks like they're leaving," I said as the men who had emerged from the plane walked up the gangplank and disappeared inside. The door closed, and the engine that had been idling revved up. The plane started to taxi to get lined up for a takeoff, and then the men from the sedan returned to their car and drove away. "So, what now?"

"I'll take you home."

"What about your car?" I asked, assuming he'd left a car back at Spade's place.

"I don't have a car."

"So how did you get to Spade's estate?"

"I was dropped off."

I wanted to ask by whom and how he planned to follow Spade without a car, but I knew he wouldn't answer. Instead, I asked about his dog, Riptide. He informed me that Riptide was with a friend. "So will you be returning to your condo?"

"I actually hadn't planned on it," Shredder answered. "I'm only on the island to confirm something which I'm pretty sure I just confirmed, and then I'll be on my way."

"Sean and Kevin are doing enchilada and margarita night," I persuaded. "And the waves are decent for June. We could get in a few runs." I looked the man up and down. "It looks like you could use some sun."

"Are you back in the condos? I heard you moved out to Luke's place."

I nodded. "Cam moved to LA, and Luke has been in Texas so long, I moved back in with Kekoa. Everyone is still around, except for Mary and Malia who moved out not long after you disappeared." I could see that Shredder was tempted, so I continued. "If you stay, we can talk about the murders. Three in twenty days. All three were men and all three were left in locations where the odds were high that I would be the one to find them. I'm not sure what this is all about, but I would welcome your input. If you come back to the condo, we can talk. Between runs, of course."

Shredder turned onto the highway that led to the condo. "Okay. I need to make a call, but I wouldn't mind a few days on the island. Is it okay if we stop and pick up Riptide?"

"Absolutely. Sandy will be thrilled to see him."

Chapter 6

As soon as I got home, I called my dad and informed him that our missing person was seen at Dillingham Airfield with two men who looked to be up to no good. Of course, once I shared this information, I had to endure a lecture about going off on my own without telling anyone where I was going. I wanted to remind him that I was his partner and not his daughter when it came to the detective agency, but I was so happy to have Shredder home, even if it was only for a few days, that I decided to let it go. Dad offered to go and have a chat with Hokulani Palakiko, so I forwarded him the photo. Now that we had technically found the guy, I supposed our job was over. We hadn't been able to return him home, but that hadn't been what the woman had hired us to do. Palakiko didn't look to be under duress. I figured he was most likely involved in some sort of illegal activity, and most likely didn't want to be found. If the men on the plane were on Shredder's radar, then the odds were they were pretty darn dangerous, and it would probably be best if Hoku left things alone.

As predicted, Sandy was thrilled to see that his old buddy, Riptide, was back, and everyone was happy to see Shredder. Shredder wanted a few minutes to make some phone calls, so I told him I'd just meet him out on the beach. I was the only one living at the condominium complex who knew about his secret life, so I was sure he was going to have to come up with one heck of a story as to why his golden brown tan had faded to a skin tone that can only be described as ghostlike when the excuse he most often used when he was away was that he'd been chasing the waves.

I checked my messages just before I tossed my cell onto my towel. There was a text from Dad, letting me know that he'd called and spoken to Hoku, and was on his way to show her the photo I had taken as proof that her husband was alive and well. I felt bad for the woman. It seemed she genuinely loved her husband, and I was sure it would be rough on her if it turned out he was wrapped up in some sort of illegal activity and ended up in prison. I supposed there could still be another explanation as to what Shredder and I had seen, and if there was even a doubt in her mind, I supposed Hoku would have to decide whether or not she wanted Dad and me to look into things further.

Grabbing my board, I headed toward the warm salty water. The waves off the condo weren't really the best, but they were adequate, and it was convenient not to have to drive anywhere for a few runs. The water felt like satin against my skin as I slowly paddled out beyond the breakers. When I'd worked as a full-time lifeguard, I'd gotten a lot of exercise. Much more than I'd needed. My job had basically consisted of me swimming out to save someone or running down the beach to handle an accident or other types of incidents on the sand. Now, my job mainly consisted of sitting around waiting for people, clues, information, or whatever was needed to wrap up a case. I still surfed most days, but I could feel the tension in my muscles. If I wanted to maintain the muscle mass and aerobic conditioning I'd spent years developing, I was going to need to up my game.

Once I'd paddled out a good distance, I turned and sat on my board. I could see Shredder and Riptide walking toward the beach, so I supposed I'd wait for him before catching the first wave. There is something so totally relaxing about bobbing gently in the sea. The steady rhythm, the sound of the waves crashing to the shore, the cooling breeze blowing in from the sea, all combined to create the perfect heaven on earth. It was times like these that I knew I would never move from my homeland. Not for Luke, not for anyone. It really was time for us to have a talk about the state of our relationship. I'd hoped to do it in person, but if he was unable to make the trip to the island as he'd hoped, I supposed a video chat would have to do.

"Man, I've missed this," Shredder said, after paddling up next to me.

"You never did say why you were gone as long as you were. You mentioned being incarcerated. Have you spent the entire nine months you were away behind bars?"

"No. I was only detained for a few weeks. I was working the rest of the time."

"Okay, so what did you do to end up being detained in the first place?"

"I can't go into the details. Let's just say that there was a slight miscommunication between myself and one of the sheik's wives that led to an unfortunate encounter between the sheik's guards and me."

"Miscommunication?" I asked.

"Let's just say she failed to disclose her marital status in a timely manner."

Figured it would be a woman who would land Shredder in hot water.

"So other than spending time in some Arab prison, what else have you been up to?"

Shredder shrugged. "Oh, you know. This and that. How about you? I assume you gave up on the idea of joining the HPD."

I took a few minutes to explain how Dad and I had worked together to find the person who'd shot Jason and almost ended his life. I shared that Dad felt we worked good together and that he realized he wasn't quite ready to fully retire, so he'd suggested the detective agency. So far, things had gone very well. We were slowly building a reputation which kept us busy, and the cases we'd handled, while mostly tame in comparison to whatever seemed to be going on with our missing person, had been satisfactorily wrapped up.

We discussed the fact that Cam had moved to LA, and Shredder admitted that he was going to miss the guy. We chatted about the other tenants of the condominium complex, and the changes they'd each gone through while Shredder had been away. We spend the next hour just catching up and never did get around to catching any waves, but we could surf anytime. Today, I just wanted to reconnect with my friend.

After we'd discussed most of the important subjects, we surfed in, and then each went our separate ways to shower and dress for dinner with Sean and Kevin. Kekoa had showered earlier, which worked out well since I was running behind. I jumped in the shower and let the cool water wash the salt from my body. I supposed I should call Dad and see how his meeting with Hoku went. It had been a case that we'd both worked on, so I should be in on the wrap up as well. I'd do it after I got dressed. I could hear Kekoa chatting with someone in the other room. Probably Elva. If I had to guess, one or both of the women had volunteered to bring dessert for the dinner party.

After washing my hair, I rinsed one more time and then turned off the water. I dried myself with the towel I'd brought in from the hall closet and then pulled on a clean pair of shorts and a fun summer t-shirt. I ran a comb through my hair, paused to make sure I'd mopped up the water that had found its way to the tile floor, and then headed toward the hamper. Once I'd deposited my soiled towel and clothing, I headed toward the small kitchen to join the women.

"Mom? I didn't realize it was you out here talking to Kekoa."

"I came by to ask if you knew where your father was. He was supposed to come with me to a benefit dinner for the arts program I work with, but he never came home, and he's not answering his cell. I hoped you might know what he was up to."

"I know he was planning to meet with one of our clients. Did you check the office?'

"I did, and he's not there." Mom looked at her watch. "I am supposed to give a speech and present the awards, so I really need to go. Kekoa said you had plans, but do you think you could track him down and remind him that he promised he would attend the benefit this evening? He keeps promising me this new business of his won't interfere with the promises he made to me to take it easy and relax after he retired, but it seems like he misses as many events as he did when he was a cop. We've had to cancel dinner with the Howards twice in two weeks. I really don't think this new hobby of his is working out at all."

I knew that Pope Investigations was a lot more than a hobby to Dad, but I didn't say as much since the last thing I wanted to do was to get in the middle of a spat between my parents. I promised my mom that I would track Dad down and remind him about the benefit. I just hoped that if he wasn't at the office by now, he was still at Hoku's home. Otherwise, I had no idea where to look for him.

"I hope I won't be long," I said to Kekoa after Mom left. "Maybe an hour at the most if Dad isn't at the office. Tell the others to save me a margarita. I've been thinking about them all day."

"Do you want me to come with you?"

"No, I'm fine. If I am going to be more than an hour, I'll text or call. I know that Dad planned to meet with Hoku, so I'm hoping that he simply got tied up trying to work out the next steps with her and lost track of time."

Luckily, the traffic wasn't too bad, so the drive to Hoku's home only took about twenty minutes. When

I pulled up in front of her house, I immediately noticed that Dad's car was parked in the drive next to Hoku's. I was a little surprised that Dad hadn't been checking his phone for messages, but he did tend to get distracted when working a case, and lately, it seemed he was more distracted than usual. I walked up the front walkway and rang the bell. When there was no answer, I knocked and rang the bell again. When there was still no answer, I tried the door, which I found to be unlocked. I opened it, stepped into the entry, and called out to announce my arrival. When there was still no response, I started down the hallway, calling out my presence as I went.

I felt the muscles in my stomach tighten with each step that I took without a reply. Surely, even if the pair was outside on the lanai, they could hear me calling out to them. "Dad," I called again. "It's Lani. Are you here?"

Still no reply.

When I arrived at the room that I knew the Palakikos used as an office, the door was closed. I slowly opened it and then gasped. "Dad!" I called out when I saw him lying unresponsive on the floor. I fully entered the room and started toward him when everything went black.

Chapter 7

Thursday, June 27

When I came to, I found myself chained to the wall of an old shed. The length of the chain was generous, so I could move around the room, but I really couldn't go anywhere. I looked toward the boarded up window. There was a gap between the board and the bottom of the window that was large enough for a limited view. It looked like the sun was just beginning to lighten the sky. The last thing I remembered was going to the home of one of our clients in search of my dad. It was evening then, and now it was early morning. Had I been here all this time?

I sat on the hard dirt floor and tried to remember how I'd gotten here. I remembered arriving at the home of Hokulani Palakiko. I remembered that no one seemed to be around, so I let myself in. I remembered walking down the hallway to the office, where I hoped to find my dad. I remembered opening the door and stepping in and — *oh god.*

Dad had been lying on the floor. He'd clearly been unconscious. I remembered trying to get to him. The next thing I remembered was waking up here. Based on the fact that the sun had not yet peaked the horizon, it was probably around five a.m. I'd arrived at the Palakiko home shortly after seven p.m. Had I really been unconscious the whole time? It seemed unlikely, but I didn't remember a single thing after a brief flash of pain as a hard object connected with the back of my skull.

I tugged at the chain around my right ankle, but it had been secured tightly. I needed to get out of here, and I needed to get help. I had no idea if Dad was dead or alive. If he'd been alive when I'd found him, would he still be alive now? I wanted to panic. I wanted to scream and cry and tug at my chain until my ankle was bloody, but I knew that wouldn't help. I needed to keep my cool and figure this out. I slowly looked around the room. Wooden walls that had decayed after years under the sun, dirt floors, a small window, which had been boarded up, allowed a thin view of the world outside. A door that looked to be newer than the walls and, if I wasn't mistaken, it was made of reinforced steel. Chances were that even if I could escape the chain around my ankle, I'd have better luck trying to pry the wood from the window than going through the door which I assumed was locked.

I did a quick search of my clothing to confirm that I was no longer in possession of my cell. Actually, now that I thought about it, I was pretty sure I left my cell in my Jeep, which the last time I'd seen it, had been parked in front of the Palakiko home.

I paused to consider the entirety of my situation. I didn't seem to have access to water, which was going to be a problem before too long. It was still early in the day, but the enclosed space was already getting hot. I tried to remember if I'd ever seen a shack such as the one I'd been imprisoned in. I could hear the sea in the distance, but other than the sea, I didn't hear anything. That told me that I wasn't close to a road. At least not a road with much traffic.

There was nothing inside the small shed except my chain, a rock, and me, so I didn't think it was currently being used for any other purpose. I had been out cold during the entire time I was being transported to this location, so I had no idea how far we'd traveled from the Palakiko home. I looked down at my ankle as the shock I'd been feeling turned to fear, and the first tears began to flow. I knew I needed to do something, both to save myself and to save my dad if he was still alive, but I had no idea what to do. Should I scream? Would that only attract the person who kidnapped me, alerting him that I was awake? If I was going to have any hope at all of getting out of here, it needed to be quick because by mid-morning this little shed would be an oven.

I knew that attempting to pry the plywood over the small window loose could very well alert my abductor that I was awake, but I also knew I needed to take that chance. I needed to find a way to circulate the stale air in the shed, and the window seemed to be the only option unless someone had actually left the door unlocked. I decided to try the door first, but couldn't quite reach it. I stretched out my body and extended my arm as far as it would go, but having a tiny body also meant I had short arms, so no matter how much I wanted to reach the door, I could see that success was not going to be an option. Heading toward the window, I stood and considered the makeshift carpentry job. A piece of plywood had been nailed to the window from the outside, so all I needed to do to remove it was to present enough force to loosen the nails. Once they were loose, I should be able to push the piece of wood onto the ground. Getting the leverage needed to loosen the nails when the window was both high on the wall and narrow, was going to be tricky.

I tried to shove at the wood for a good fifteen minutes before I realized I was both tiring myself out and getting nowhere. I was certain the nails holding the plywood would give if I had enough oomph behind my movements to push the board away from the window, but it wasn't like I could really push with my legs. I needed to get the dang chain off my ankle so I could walk around freely, but short of cutting off my foot, which even if I had been brave enough to do, I had no tool to do so with, I really had no way to get free. Then it occurred to me that if I couldn't free my ankle from the chain, maybe I could figure out a way to free the chain from the wall.

Deciding to focus my energy there, I left the window and made my way to the wall. The chain was attached to a ring that had been bolted to the wall. The bolts looked to be tighter than I could unscrew with my fingers alone, and I didn't have any tools to help me, but I did have a rock, so maybe if I pounded on the ring that was attached to the wall, it would loosen up a bit. I had no way of knowing if this would work but decided I had nothing to lose by trying. If I did nothing, it seemed fairly apparent that I would die.

When I hit the ring on the wall with the rock, the chain vibrated, causing the cuff around my ankle to dig into my already tender skin. I stiffed a scream before gritting my teeth and hitting the ring in the wall once again. I tried over and over again as blood ran from my ankle down over my bare foot. In spite of my continued effort, it didn't seem like anything was happening. I didn't see any other option of freeing myself, so I continued to hit the ring with the rock in spite of the pain, and eventually, I noticed that the bolt began to loosen just a bit. I continued to pound on the ring in spite of the damage it was doing to my ankle, and eventually, the bolt loosened enough that I was able to unscrew the ring and get the chain free.

Of course, the cuff was still around my ankle, and the chain was still attached to the cuff. Trying to escape while dragging a chain was not going to be easy.

Now that I was no longer attached to the wall, I turned my attention to the need to get out of the room. I tried the door I had previously been unable to reach to confirm that it was indeed locked, and then I turned my attention to the window. As I'd already determined, it was high and narrow and boarded from the outside. My only tool was my rock, but if I could get some height, that might be enough to do the job. I also had the long chain that was still secured to my ankle. Now that I was no longer attached to the wall, I realized I might be able to use it as a tool as well.

I sat down on the floor and looked at the cuff around my ankle. I really didn't see any way of getting it loose, and the chain that was attached to it seemed pretty secure as well. The chain was sturdy, but not overly bulky. It looked to be long enough to use as a rope if I was able to toss it up and over the beam that seemed to support the A-frame rafters, which supported the roof of the wooden building. It would be tricky to get it up and over the beam without injuring my ankle any more than it already was, but I really had no other option, so I knew I had to try. Taking a deep breath, I used all of my strength to toss the chain up and over the beam. Once I'd accomplished that, I tied off the end not attached to my leg and then praying the knot would hold and the whole thing would support my weight, I climbed up it like a rope. Once I was the same height as the window, I used my feet to push off from the wall, and then when I swung back, I angled myself so that my unchained foot came into contact with the board covering the window. When contact was made, I heard the board give just a bit, so I regrouped and tried it again and again. Eventually, the board gave way enough that I could pry it loose and push it to the ground. It was a small opening, but I was a small woman, so I pulled the chain down from the overhead rafter and let it trail behind me. I pulled myself up toward the window, flattened myself out, and squeezed through. Once I was on the ground, I pulled the rest of my chain through.

My ankle, which was still attached to the chain, was raw and bleeding, and my feet weren't in much better shape. My hands were scraped raw in places from all my escape efforts. I had no shoes, so walking on the rough ground wouldn't be easy, but staying where I was wasn't an option. I surveyed the jungle surrounding me and tried to imagine where I was. I could see the sea in the distance, so I decided to head in that direction. I knew that I'd eventually come across a road.

I took off my t-shirt and tore it in half. I wrapped one-half of the bright yellow top around each of my feet. I tied them as securely as I could, and then I wrapped the chain around my waist and up over my shoulder. Walking with the weight of the chain was going to make things even more difficult, but until I could find a way to free myself from it, that was what I would need to do. I gritted my teeth and dug down deep for the determination I'd need before setting off down the mountain in a pair of ripped and bloody shorts and a bra.

As I walked, the jungle became thick with close-growing trees and untamed underbrush. The dense foliage made maintaining a direction tough, but it also provided shade, which I would need to endure the heat of the day without shelter or water.

Each step was a struggle, but I knew what I had to do, so I continued one painful step at a time. Once I was a good distance away from the shed, I paused to consider the scenery once again. I could no longer see the sea in the distance, but I figured as long as I continued to head downhill, I should eventually find it, and the odds were, once I found the sea, I'd find a road.

After I had been hiking for an hour or more, I paused to listen. I could hear a hum in the distance. It could be traffic noise from a road, but my intuition told me that I'd found a fall. I changed direction just a bit and headed toward the sound. When I saw the tall falls pouring into a crystal clear pool of water, I wanted to cry. Suddenly, I knew exactly where I was.

The cool, clear water was heaven against my skin. I unwound the chain from my body and the t-shirt from my feet, and slowly slid into the water. I sunk down to my neck, and let the water cool my skin and cleanse my wounds. By this point, my feet were so far gone that I knew it would be a good long while before I would be able to walk comfortably again, but at least I believed I would live. I sat on the bottom of the shallow pond, staying close to the edge. I felt the tension in my neck and shoulders melt away as I closed my eyes and tried to figure out my next move. I needed to let someone know about my father. I had no cell, and it was at least a two-mile hike from the falls to the road. Given the state of my feet, and the fact I was carrying a long and heavy chain, it would take more than an hour to travel that two miles, but it seemed that was the only option I had. I supposed it was possible that I might run into hikers on their way up to the falls, but it was still really early in the day, so that seemed sort of unlikely.

As wonderful as the water felt on my feet, I knew I needed to continue on my way, so I pulled myself out of the pool of water and found a large rock to sit on. Once I'd dried off a bit, I began to wrap my bloody and muddy t-shirt around my feet once again. I'd been totally focused on the painful task, and only heard a noise behind me an instant before someone put a hand over my mouth. I tried to scream, but all that came out was a muffled oomph.

"It's me," Shredder said into my ear. "Don't make a sound. There are men looking for you. They are not far behind us."

I nodded to let him know I understood.

Shredder took his hand from my mouth. He gathered up my chain and then picked me up in his arms. Once I was settled against his chest, he headed into the jungle. I wrapped my arms around his neck and held on as he moved efficiently and silently through the dense foliage. Eventually, he paused and set me down on a large rock. He took out a pair of binoculars and looked around.

"How did you find me?" I whispered.

"I'll tell you later. Right now, we need to lose the guys who are tracking you. Now be quiet."

I nodded again.

After a few minutes, Shredder picked me up again and headed further into the jungle away from the sea. That made no sense to me. The road where we could find help was downhill, yet Shredder was traveling uphill. Shredder was a big guy, and I was a small woman, but I still didn't see how he was going to be able to carry my chain and me too far if we continued to climb the way we were. I wanted to question the direction he was taking, but he'd told me to be quiet, so I supposed I'd be quiet. He was, after all, some sort of superspy, while I was just me. I had to believe he had a strategy for heading uphill rather than down.

After we'd traveled for quite a while, he stopped at a small stream. He gently set me down and, once again, pulled out his binoculars. I waited for him to survey the situation. Eventually, he looked down at me. "Are you okay?"

"A little worse for wear, but I'll live. My dad..."

"In the hospital."

I let out a breath of relief. "Is he okay?"

"He will be."

"How did you find me?" I still couldn't imagine that he had.

"The shack where you were being held is located on an estate owned by a man named Mikayo Tatsuo. I recognized him as one of the men on the plane piloted by Kinsley Palakiko yesterday. When you never showed up at the dinner last night, Kekoa began to get worried. When she told me where you'd gone, I went to check it out, only to find your dad unconscious on the floor. Your car was on the street in front of the house, but you were nowhere to be found, so Jason and I went looking for you. We were hitting dead end after dead end until I remembered the meeting between Tatsuo and Spade. On a hunch, I checked to see if Tatsuo owned property on the island. He actually owns quite a bit. Nine houses, four warehouses, and the estate where I eventually stumbled upon a group of men who seemed to be looking for someone. I followed them into the jungle and continued to follow them until I figured out where you would most likely head. Then, I circled around and managed to get in front of them. By the time I found you at the falls, they were less than a quarter of a mile away."

I tucked my damp hair behind my ear. "I guess I should be thanking you right about now."

"No thanks necessary. Right now, we need to focus on getting out of here. Tatsuo's men continued to travel downhill toward the highway. I doubt they'll pick up our trail at this point, but we do need to make our way back." Shredder took out a device that looked like a cross between a phone and walkie-talkie. "I should be able to call Jason and let him know what is going on once we make our way out of the jungle. I seem to remember there being a clearing not far from here." Shredder reached down and picked me up once again. "If my memory is correct, it should be less than a half a mile away."

Once we reached the clearing, Shredder used his phone, which I assumed was some sort of a satellite phone, to call Jason, who told us to sit tight and wait for a helicopter to pick us up. Shredder moved us out of the open space to wait. The temperature was beginning to climb, but there was a cool crosswind that made things bearable even though we were quite a distance from the sea.

"So what do you think is going on?" I asked after we'd both settled in under a grouping of tall trees.

"Tatsuo is one of those untouchable businessmen who everyone knows is wrapped up in illegal activities but is smart enough to avoid an evidence trail. He owns multiple pieces of property in Hawaii, Los Angeles, and Hong Kong. I've been tracking him since I received a tip that he has expanded his market and is now dealing in human trafficking, mainly young women he brings into the States from Asia. So far, I have been unable to prove any of this. Tatsuo is well protected, and getting close to him is near impossible. A few weeks ago, I got a tip that Tatsuo was working with Spade on his latest venture, so I decided to approach things from a different angle and watch Spade."

"Which is why you were at the estate yesterday."

"Exactly. I hoped that by following Spade, I could confirm the link with Tatsuo, which I hoped would lead me to some sort of proof relating to the human trafficking tip that, of course, no one will admit to. The meeting at the airport yesterday confirmed my suspicion that the two are working together. My plan was to confirm Spade's involvement and then go back to tracking Tatsuo. Now, I'm not so sure if that is the right move. I have no reason to believe that Spade or Tatsuo know I am here, but they obviously know that both you and your dad are somehow involved with Palakiko. In my opinion, that puts you both in danger."

"You think Tatsuo will send his men to kill us?"

"Honestly, I don't know why both you and your father aren't already dead. There must be a piece to this puzzle that is still missing."

"What about Mrs. Palakiko?" I asked. "Has she been found?"

Shredder informed me that at the time he came to look for me, she hadn't been found and that he suspected either Tatsuo or Spade were detaining her to provide the leverage they needed to ensure that Kinsley did exactly what they wanted him to do. I was about to ask him about his next move when the chopper appeared on the horizon. I supposed the conversation could wait until I'd had a chance to remove my chain, bandage my feet, and check on my dad.

"Wait here, and I'll get something to remove that chain," Shredder said, as the chopper landed in the clearing.

As I watched Shredder run toward the whirling blades, I finally let myself believe that my ordeal was over. If only I'd known at the time that, in reality, my ordeal, as well as Shredder's, was only just beginning.

Chapter 8

Jason met us at the airport. Once the helicopter landed, he shuffled me off to the hospital before I could argue. I hadn't planned to make such a fuss over a few minor scrapes and abrasions. I figured I could clean and bandage them myself, but Jason had a different idea. I wondered if Shredder would come with us, but he didn't. He gave me a hard hug and told me that we would talk later that evening. It seemed he had things to follow up on that really couldn't wait, but he was sure that Jason would take good care of me. I was sure he would as well if he didn't smother me in the process.

"So tell me exactly what happened," Jason asked, as we drove toward the hospital.

I rolled down the window and let the wind blow through my hair. "There isn't much to tell. Mom came by my condo looking for Dad yesterday around seven. I guess he was supposed to accompany her to some benefit but had never shown up, and she wondered if I knew where he might be. I told her that the last I heard, he had gone over to Hokulani Palakiko's house to let her know that we'd found her husband."

"I spoke to Shredder after he found Dad knocked out in the Palakiko home, and he told me Mr. Palakiko had been piloting a plane carrying two men who had come to the island to speak to Spade."

"That's right. I'm not really sure what that was all about. I didn't notice the men exchange anything other than conversation, so it would seem that if all you wanted to do was talk, why not call or email or even text a message?"

"I'm sure they had their reasons for a face to face interview. Go on."

I rolled up the window and turned up the air conditioner. "Anyway, when I arrived at the Palakiko home, I saw Dad's car in the drive. I went up to the door and knocked, but there was no answer. I let myself in and found Dad unconscious on the floor. I started toward him, and then everything went black. The next thing I knew, it was a new day, and I was chained to a wall in an old shed."

A look of concern crossed Jason's face. "You were unconscious from yesterday evening until this morning?"

"Yes. I guess I was." I put a hand to my head. "That's strange right? I mean, I don't even have a headache. I did feel somewhat groggy when I first came to, but that has passed."

"I am going to guess you were drugged. After Dad was taken to the hospital, they found a puncture wound in his neck. He was unconscious for hours before he was found."

"Is he okay?"

"He is. They want to keep him at the hospital overnight for observation. They may want to keep you as well."

"I'm not staying overnight. I will allow them to clean and wrap my injured feet, but then I am gone. Agreed?"

Jason looked like he was going to argue, but then he seemed to stop himself. "Agreed." He pulled into a nearby parking area. "So other than the fact that you were knocked out and imprisoned, do you remember anything else? Do you know why you were kidnapped?"

"I don't know. Shredder told me that one of the men we saw at the airport yesterday owns the estate where I was held. I suppose that this whole thing must tie back to whatever is going on with Kinsley Palakiko since I was taken from his house and he was piloting the plane carrying the men Spade met with."

"Do you know the name of the man who owns the estate where Shredder found you?"

"Mikayo Tatsuo."

"Did you see the face of any of the men who kidnapped you at any point?" Jason asked.

"No. Shredder saw the men who were tracking me after I escaped if you are looking for someone to provide descriptions. I didn't see who knocked me out, and I was alone when I came to. I worked myself free and left before anyone came looking for me. I didn't see anyone other than Shredder the entire time."

Jason pulled into a parking space. "Okay. Let's get you checked out. We can check on Dad after that and then I'll take you home. I need you to promise me that you will take it easy for a few days and that you will not do any investigating on your own."

"I'll take it easy. I'll even call my boss at the resort and let him know I won't be in on Saturday."

"I noticed you didn't agree to the no investigating," Jason pointed out.

I just smiled. We both knew that no investigating was something I'd never agree to.

The cleaning and wrapping of my wounds turned out to be a fairly quick and painless undertaking. I was given a mild pain medication and an antibiotic as a preventative measure, and my blood test confirmed that I had indeed been drugged with a sedative, most likely delivered directly to my neck which is where they found a small puncture wound. When Jason and I went to visit Dad, we found him awake and chomping at the bit to be released. Of course, he had Mom to deal with, and she was having none of it.

"I'm so relieved that you are okay," Dad hugged me from his hospital bed. "When I came to after Shredder found me and I realized your car was at the house, but you were nowhere to be found, I nearly had a heart attack."

"Things did appear sort of dicey for a while this morning, but I'm fine, and I think we actually came out of this with new information."

"Your dad needs to rest, so there will be no shop talk," Mom, who was sitting in a chair next to the bed, interrupted.

I glanced at Mom. "Sorry. You're right. Jason and I just wanted to check in, but we should be going." I turned and looked at Dad. "Call me after you are released and we'll catch up."

Dad didn't look happy about the situation, but he didn't argue either. I hugged both my parents one more time and then left with my brother. Walking on my bandaged feet was somewhat uncomfortable, but the hospital had provided me with large open-air shoes, much like Crocs, which provided a sole to offer protection and support, yet also provided plenty of room for the bandages. I wanted to grill Jason to find out if he knew anything I didn't about Tatsuo, Palakiko, or any of our three murder victims who my instinct told me were all involved in the same thing, but I could tell by the look on his face that he just wanted me home safe and not digging around in what was clearly a police matter, so I decided to play it cool and chat with him about his wife and two children as we made the drive to my condo.

"So any idea what happened to my Jeep?" I asked after we pulled up in front of the condo, and I realized it wasn't in my parking space.

"I'll check on it. It might still be on the street in front of the Palakiko home."

"I'm going to need transportation, so if you could check on it sooner rather than later, that would be great," I offered my brother a big smile.

"To be honest, I'm tempted to have the dang thing impounded so you will be forced to stay put."

"Impounding my Jeep won't keep me from doing what I need to do, but it will make me mad. I'm not a baby. I don't need my big brother managing my life."

Jason blew out a breath. "I know. You are the most capable woman I know. I'll have your Jeep brought to you within the hour. Just be careful. I love you. I would die if something happened to you."

I reached across the seat between us and took Jason's hand in mine. "I know. I love you too. And I will be careful. In fact, my plan for today includes a shady spot on the lanai and a tall glass of iced tea."

"That sounds perfect."

Jason helped me into the condo where Kekoa and Elva were waiting for me. It looked like being nursed and fussed over was going to be part of my day no matter how much I wished otherwise. I knew that my cousin and neighbor loved me, and I knew they'd been worried about me, but I really wasn't the sort to want all the attention that came with the package.

"I was so worried." Kekoa wrapped her arms around me the minute I walked in the door.

"I'm fine." I hugged her back. "A little banged up, but fine."

"And Uncle Keanu?"

"He is fine as well. The hospital is going to keep him overnight as a precaution, but he seemed totally fine. I'm sure he'll be back to work by next week." I headed to the refrigerator and grabbed a soda. "So how was the party?"

"Great until I realized that you had been gone a lot longer than you should have been. When I couldn't get ahold of you, of course, I panicked. I guess it was a good thing I knew where you were headed."

"It was. You might very well have saved my life. Shredder would never have known to come to look for me if you hadn't decided to check on me."

"He would have missed you eventually as well."

"Perhaps, but let's not worry about what happened yesterday and focus on today. I'm starving.

I never did get dinner last night, and I haven't eaten today."

"I know the guys had leftover enchiladas. I would be willing to bet they could be persuaded to share."

"I'll go and ask them," Elva offered.

"And I'll grab the tequila," Kekoa joined in. "You can't have enchiladas without margaritas."

Chapter 9

By the time Shredder arrived at the condo, the five residents on the premises were well fed and happy. Normally, I would have immediately pulled Shredder aside to grill him about what he knew, but today I was just so happy that we were all together, I found myself greeting him with an icy drink rather than a bunch of questions. Of course, we both knew that the questions would come later, but for now, I was going to take my brother's advice and take it easy.

"You look better," Shredder said after I handed him a drink.

"The hospital took care of my injuries, a cool shower took care of my itchiness, and this margarita took care of the rest." I glanced down at the clunky shoes I had on. "I won't be making any fashion statements for the next few days, and I have to stay out of the sea for ten days, which is frustrating, but I'm going to be fine thanks to you."

"I'm glad I was here to provide the rescue." Shredder smiled. "I really hadn't realized how much I'd missed this place until I was back. It's going to be hard to leave again."

"So don't leave. You just got here, and we missed you."

"I have a job to do."

"Perhaps, but you seem to have some pull with the people you work with. Just tell them you need a break and are taking some time off."

"If only it were that easy."

My smile faded just a bit. Shredder was the sort to put his responsibilities first, and I knew he would go as abruptly as he'd shown up. "Are you leaving soon?"

"Not yet. I want to make sure that whatever is going on here is all wrapped up before I leave. We really should go over things again. I feel like there are a lot of pieces that don't really seem to fit. I also know that you have been working on it for a while. If I know you, which I do, I suspect that you are already honing in on the missing piece or pieces."

I loved the fact that Shredder wanted to consult with me and actually seemed to value my input. "Do you want to talk now?"

"Let me grab a bite to eat, and then maybe we can go next door and talk where it is quieter."

After Shredder downed two chicken and two beef enchiladas, we told the others we were going to head over to his condo so he could show me the surfing videos he had taken while he was away. As far as I knew, Kevin, Sean, and Elva all believed he actually did spend his time chasing the waves, although, with the pasty white skin he had returned to Hawaii with, I didn't know how they could believe that. I was pretty sure that Kekoa suspected there was actually more to his story, but, as I already mentioned, I was the only one living at the complex who knew the extent of his secret.

"So here is what we know," Shredder began after we were both seated. "Three men have been murdered in the past three weeks. All three were killed in a location other than the site where the body was dumped, and all three dump sites seem to coordinate to a location where the likelihood of you finding the body would be significant. None of the locations where the bodies were dumped are exclusive to you, however, which means that while the killer seems to prefer that you find the body, your finding it isn't really critical to whatever is going on."

"I agree. While it seems like the killer wanted to create a link between the men who were murdered and me, there is no way he or she could know that someone else wouldn't stumble across the bodies before I did, so the actual discoveries of the bodies by me must be less important than establishing the link." I paused to let this really sink in. "Any idea why the killer wanted to involve me at all? These men weren't our clients. Hokulani Palakiko hired us to find her husband, but the other three men, the men who were murdered, wouldn't have been on my radar if I hadn't found the bodies. My involvement seems to be intentional, but I really don't know why. I didn't know these men. I wasn't invested in their lives or their deaths. Why bring me into the equation at all?"

"That is actually a really good question. Maybe if we can find a link between the three men, we can figure out how you fit into it. I have been looking into things since you told me about the murders, and I have a general idea of who each of your three murder victims was. On the surface, it doesn't seem that the three men are linked in any way, but if you dig deeper, connections begin to appear."

"I agree. Dad and I spoke to the cousin of the last victim who owned a food truck. He told us that before he died, Ano had been seen speaking to the same woman who we found out that Walter Evans met up with at the Dolphin Bay Resort. The woman checked into the resort under the name Samantha Jones, but according to Dad, it looks like that is a fake name. I don't know if there is a link between Samantha Jones and the nightclub owner, Vinnie Travano, but there does seem to be a link between Vinnie and Spade. And, of course, as we know, Spade seems to be working with Mikayo Tatsuo in some way, and it looks as if Kinsley Palakiko is working for Tatsuo. While there aren't enough clear-cut relationships to definitively say that Kinsley Palakiko, Walter Evans, Vinnie Travano, and Ano Hanale are all connected to the same person or organization, it is beginning to look that way. Although, I have no idea why the three men turned up dead, and I have to wonder if Kinsley Palakiko won't end up being victim number four."

"I think we need to track down this Samantha Jones. It sounds like she might have one or two of the missing pieces. If nothing else, she can probably fill in a few of the blanks relating to Walter Evans and Ano Hanale."

"I can find out if she is still at the resort."

"Okay. Why don't you check on that while I make a phone call? If she is at the resort, maybe we can get her to meet us for a drink. It's still early, so she might be willing."

"She might be willing to meet for a drink, but I doubt she'll be willing to tell us what she knows, if she does, in fact, know anything."

Shredder grinned. "Generally speaking, I can be pretty persuasive."

I bet he could at that with his bad boy looks and sweet, sweet smile.

Since I worked at the resort, I knew everyone, so a call to the front desk netted me the information that Samantha Jones was still staying at the resort and that she had nine o'clock reservations at the restaurant. It was only around seven now, so I figured if Shredder really wanted to speak to her, we could change into something appropriate for the restaurant and arrange to bump into the woman as she arrived or perhaps as she left the facility after finishing her meal. Of course, we had no way to know if she was alone or with another person or even a group, so I supposed our best bet was just to head to the resort and play it by ear.

Shredder liked my plan, so I changed into a dress. There wasn't a lot I could do with my feet since they were bandaged the way they were, but I did find a pair of sandals that were more attractive than the clogs the hospital had given me. The bandages on my hands seemed unnecessary now that the bleeding was under control, so I took them off and hoped they didn't look so gross that everyone would be staring at them. Perhaps once we got to the resort, I should allow Shredder to speak to Samantha alone. I was afraid that my cuts and abrasions, along with the bandages on my feet, would make her suspicious right off the bat. I mentioned this to Shredder, and he agreed. He gave me an earpiece so I could listen in on his conversation. Jason would have told me to wait in the car and not get in the way, but Shredder was treating me like a partner. I liked that.

Chapter 10

Samantha Jones was stunning. Long black hair, a tall thin frame, perfectly tanned skin, and dark eyes that were as alluring as they were mysterious. When we first arrived at the resort, we found Samantha in the bar having a drink with a dark-haired, dark-skinned gentleman, who looked to be in his early fifties. Shredder didn't recognize the man, so he took a photo of him and sent it off to whomever he was working with. Once that was done, Shredder entered the open-air bar and took a seat several stools down from where Samantha and the man were discussing paddleboard races. There didn't seem to be anything sinister about that, so I had to assume the man she was with was simply someone she ran into while stopping to have a pre-dinner drink. Confirming my suspicion, Samantha remained after the man left. Shredder lifted a glass in greeting, and Samantha waved him over. He ordered another round and asked about her day. Since Shredder wore a wire, I could hear everything he could. I looked around and found a hiding place behind a giant Tiki statue. I had a decent line of sight, although I was mostly looking at everyone's back, except for those occasions when someone would turn and look away from the bar toward the larger seating area beyond the bar.

"So where are you visiting from?" Shredder asked the woman, I assumed as a means of entering into a conversation.

"Actually, I am between homes, but I have business on the North Shore, so I'm staying at the resort for a few weeks. How about you? Based on your lack of tan, I assume you are not a local."

"I'm actually a private investigator. I'm on the island to look into the deaths of Walter Evans, Vinnie Travano, and Ano Hanale. I understand that you met with Evans prior to his death. I hoped you would be willing to tell me what you know about the man."

"So this meeting wasn't a random event?"

"No. I'm afraid not. So how about it? Maybe we could have another drink and discuss the matter."

The woman didn't answer right away. Since I couldn't see her face, I wasn't able to read her expression, so I wasn't sure if she was thinking things over or if she had simply clammed up. Shredder didn't speak either. He seemed to be waiting her out. After a full minute, she finally spoke. "I might know a thing or two, but I can't discuss what I know here. I might be able to help you, however, if you are willing to come back to my private cottage."

"I would be willing to do that."

"I was supposed to meet someone for dinner, but I'll cancel and just have food brought to my room.

Oh, and lose the wire. Anything discussed between us will need to stay between us."

"Can you give me a minute?"

"I can give you several minutes." The woman borrowed a pen from the bartender and jotted something down on a napkin. She passed the napkin to Shredder and then got up and walked away. Talk about anti-climactic.

"You heard?" Shredder asked.

"I heard."

"I'm going to need to lose the wire, so you won't be able to listen in. I would suggest you take the Jeep and head home, but I know you can't drive until your feet have healed a bit. I can call you a car."

"I'll just wait here in the bar. I know the bartender. If it gets too late, I'll have Kekoa come and get me. It's frustrating not to be able to listen in, but I get it."

"I know, but the woman is obviously a professional. I don't know how she knew someone was listening in, but she did. I don't want to risk her clamming up." Shredder glanced at the clock. "Hopefully, I won't be long. I'll be in cottage number four."

"It's at the end of the first row of cottages closest to the beach."

"I'll try to hurry. If you get tired of waiting and decide to leave, just text me and let me know."

"Okay. Be careful."

Shredder smiled. "This isn't my first rodeo."

I grinned back. "I know, but be careful all the same."

After Shredder left, I went into the bar, sat down at the counter, and ordered a drink.

"What happened to you?" asked the bartender, whose name was Steve.

"Misadventures in hiking. Seems like a slow night for June."

"It's been slow ever since they opened the nightclub at the resort down the road. Personally, I'd prefer an open-air bar overlooking the water, but it seems that quite a few of our guests are heading down the road for the nightlife and it has really cut into our bottom line."

"I know the management of the resort has been talking about the idea of a nightclub, but I think the majority agree that the atmosphere they want to offer to our guests is one of peaceful reflection. In my opinion, the whole nightclub vibe doesn't seem to fit."

"I don't disagree, but it is hurting business. I've heard rumors that the management is working on its own version of the sort of club that went in down the road."

"In my opinion, a club would ruin the environment the management at Dolphin Bay had created, but I supposed keeping up with the current trends was always an issue."

Steve nodded in agreement. "By the way, I heard that Kekoa quit."

"She did. I guess you heard that she didn't get the promotion she was expecting."

"I heard, and I agree it should have gone to her. I'm sorry she is gone, but I don't blame her for quitting. In this day and age, you need to look out for yourself. In fact, no one knows this yet, but I might be on my way out as well."

"Are you leaving the island?"

Steve shrugged. "I might be. There is a woman staying here who told me she could hook me up with a job that will pay triple what I am making now."

I raised a brow. "Would this woman's name be Samantha?"

"It is. Do you know her?"

"Not really, but I know who she is. She's been staying here for quite a while. Several weeks it seems."

"She seems to be here on business of some sort. She's met with a lot of different men since she's been with us. I'm not exactly sure what she does, but it seems like she is some sort of a recruiter."

I pulled a photo of Walter Evans out of my purse. "Do you remember if she met with this man?"

Steve took the photo. "Yeah, he was one of the first men I saw her with, although I think they'd already been working together. I overheard part of their conversation, and it sounded like the guy is a pilot who has been working with Samantha providing private transportation for those in need of it. From what I could tell, the gig took the man all over the world."

"I suppose that being a pilot could be exciting."

Steve shrugged. "I guess, although to be honest, the vibe I picked up on wasn't one of excitement but one of secrecy. I could be wrong since I only heard snippets of the conversation, but it seemed as if the guy Samantha was with actually had a contract with someone to ferry passengers between Hong Kong, Honolulu, and LA under the radar."

"Under the radar?" I asked.

"I'm guessing he was going to sneak folks who didn't have proper paperwork into the country, although as I already said, I really only heard snippets of the conversation. It wasn't like I could linger for too long. That would have been obvious."

"Yeah, I get that." Shredder had told me that Tatsuo was dealing in human trafficking. It would seem he would need a pilot who could get those women into the country without detection. If I had to guess, the guy had access to his own plane and a private airstrip. Assuming Evans agreed to take the job, I had to wonder how he ended up dead. It sounded like he had been working with Samantha for a while, but maybe the guy had his limits. Maybe he tried to back out once he realized exactly who he'd be transporting. That would get him dead, but why had his body been left for me to find? That part still didn't make sense.

Next, I slipped a photo of Vinnie Travano across the bar. "Do you recognize this man?'

"Sure, that's Vinnie Travano. He recently died, but he used to own a nightclub on the South Shore." Steve looked up at me. "Aren't you the one who found the guy propped up on your lifeguard tower?"

"I am. I'm just trying to find out if he was linked to Walter Evans in any way."

"Not that I know of. Vinnie has been hanging around, and I've seen him talking to members of the senior staff, but I don't remember him speaking directly to Samantha. Of course, I'm not around all the time, so they may have met at some point."

I was about to ask Steve if he had seen Ano with Samantha when Shredder walked in. "That was fast."

"I got everything I was going to get and got out. Are you ready, or do you want to finish your drink?"

"I'm ready." I passed some money to Steve. "If you do decide to quit, text me a contact number. I'd like to stay in touch."

"I will. Have a good night now."

I waited until we were driving back to the condos before filling Shredder in on what I'd learned. Other than to confirm the fact that Samantha had hired Walter to pilot her clients between countries undetected, I didn't have a lot.

"Samantha confirmed that she recruited Walter to provide air service for those needing to travel discretely. They'd been working together for a while, which I imagine accounts for all the travel he has been linked to. Most recently, she hired him to provide transportation for Tatsuo. Initially, it looked like any other job, but Walter had a problem with the arrangement after he found out that his cargo consisted of women who had been kidnapped. When Evans found out that his passengers were not heading to LA willingly, he quit. Samantha suspects that it was Tatsuo or a paid assassin that killed him, but she has no evidence to back that up."

"And Vinnie?"

"She said that she'd met Vinnie briefly when he was here to speak to the Dolphin Bay Resort's management team, but she hadn't been working with him."

"And Ano?"

"I don't know," Shredder answered. "When I asked about him, Samantha said she didn't know him. When I told her that we had a witness that had seen her with Ano before he died, she insisted my witness was mistaken. I don't know why she would tell me everything she knew about Evans and then clam up when it came to Ano, but I think we need to dig deeper. The answer to that question might actually tell us a lot."

"I agree. It does seem like Tatsuo is behind most, if not all, of what is going on. I still don't know why the bodies were left for me, but I suppose we are getting closer to figuring that out as well."

The conversation stalled as Shredder pulled into my parking spot at the condo.

"Did Samantha happen to know anything about Mrs. Palakiko?" I asked.

"She hadn't heard that she was missing, but she did say that if Tatsuo has her, she is probably dead or would be dead soon. She didn't think the man would mess around with a hostage for any length of time."

"If she is alive, we need to find her."

Shredder got out of the Jeep. I slipped out of the passenger side.

"I have an idea to find out if she is dead or alive, but this is something you can't be involved in." Shredder walked me to my door and kissed my cheek. "I'll talk to you in the morning. Hopefully, by then, we'll know one way or the other."

Chapter 11

Friday, June 28

Normally, Friday would be a workday at Pope Investigations, followed by Saturday at the Dolphin Bay Resort, and then a day off on Sunday, but this weekend, between the doctor imposed instruction to stay out of the sea and Dad being in the hospital, it looked like I was going to have the full long weekend off. It had been a while since I'd had even two days off in a row, so in spite of the fact that I wasn't thrilled about the reason for my free time, I decided I was going to enjoy it to the fullest extent possible.

"Are you going somewhere?" I asked Kekoa after emerging from my bedroom to find two suitcases sitting near the front door.

"LA. Cam called last night, and we had a long talk. I tried to break things off nice and clean so we could both move on, but he convinced me to come to LA so we could talk in person before ending things completely. I no longer have my job at Dolphin Bay to worry about, and I knew Pope Investigations would be closed for a few days while you and your dad heal from your ordeals, so against my better judgment, I found myself agreeing to a short visit."

"Against your better judgment?" I asked.

Kekoa let out a long, tortured breath. "I know it's over. Over really is the only place for us to go at this point. I love Cam, but Cam loves his job, and I don't want to live in LA, so no matter how you slice it, there really isn't a future for us. I think we should just say goodbye and be done with it. It seems like spending time with Cam will only make it harder to do what I know needs to be done. Every time I see him, I am reminded of how great things used to be. I am reminded of the plans we made that will never be realized. The whole thing is just so depressing, but Cam insists that our relationship is too important to end with a phone call. He made a fairly compelling case that after everything we've had together, we owe ourselves a face to face conversation. I know this trip will only bring pain to my life, but somehow he managed to convince me to do it anyway."

I hugged my cousin. "I'm so sorry, and I totally understand what you are saying. Seeing him is going to make it harder. Still, I guess this visit will give you the opportunity to say what you need to say in order to have closure."

"I guess. I'll probably be a soggy mess by the time I get back."

"I'll stock up on tissues and wine."

Kekoa grabbed her keys from the peg. "Are you going to be okay on your own? With your injuries and all."

"I'm fine."

"Sean and Kevin leave today for a two-week shift with the airline so they won't be around either."

"Shredder will be here, and if I need something, I can always go to Elva."

Kekoa slipped the strap of her purse over her shoulder. "Okay, then I won't worry about you." She hugged me. "Take it easy while I am away and don't overdo."

"Yes, mother. And try to have fun. Try to use these days to do what needs to be done so you can move on if that is what you are sure you need to do."

"It is, and I will."

After Kekoa left, I made a pot of coffee, clipped a collar on Sandy, and took a full mug out onto the lanai. Sandy looked longingly toward the beach, but there would be no surfing or long leisurely walk today. I tossed a ball which sent my lab running. It was a beautiful morning: warm, but not hot, with a nice breeze to keep things cool. Sandy returned with the ball, so I tossed it again. I knew he could do this all day, and it was a way to get him the exercise he needed while my feet mended. I hoped I'd be back to my old self sooner rather than later. It had been less than twenty-four hours since I'd had them treated, but they already felt a hundred percent better than they had when Shredder had first found me.

Putting my feet up on a stool, I leaned back in my chair. It was quite this morning. With unit three still empty and Carina from unit four all but living with her fiancé, the place was quieter overall than it once had been. Sean and Kevin were away more often than they were home, and until the past couple of days, Shredder had been gone for months. Elva was the consistent neighbor. She rarely went anywhere and was always happy to sit and chat with Kekoa and me. With Elva around, we never felt alone.

"Morning, Lani. How are your feet?" Elva asked, after sitting down next to me.

"Much better actually. I won't be able to jog or surf or resume physical activities for a while, but I am able to walk without pain today, so that's something."

"That is something. I guess if Shredder hadn't found you, things might have been a whole lot worse."

"Yes, they very well might have been." I tossed the ball for Sandy again. "So what are you up to on this beautiful day?"

"Actually, I'm going to Maui for the weekend."

I raised a brow. "Really? Are you visiting a friend?"

She nodded. "One of the women I play bingo with has a daughter who lives on Maui. The daughter just had a baby, so she is going for a visit and invited me to come along. It's just for a few days. She is picking me up in a little while, and we'll be home Monday evening, but I'm excited about it. It's been a while since I've been anywhere."

"Well, I hope you have a wonderful time. Take photos of this new baby to share with all of us when you get home."

"I will." Elva looked up. "I guess I should finish packing. I just wanted to let you know my plans, so you didn't worry when you noticed I was gone."

"I appreciate that. And yes, I would have worried."

Elva smiled at me. "It's nice that we look out for each other that way."

It was nice, I realized. I had a mother with whom I shared a good relationship, but in many ways, Elva was like a second mother to me. I spent a lot more time with her than I did with my own mother, and if I really stopped to think about it, she knew a lot more about my life than almost anyone, except Kekoa.

After Elva went inside, I glanced toward Shredder's condo. It looked like it would be just the two of us for a few days, provided he stayed on the island for a few more days as he indicated he would. I supposed that might be for the best. By digging around the way we were, I had to assume we'd made ourselves targets and I'd hate for anyone to get caught in the crossfire if things turned ugly.

I had to admit to being curious as to what Shredder had found out after dropping me off the previous afternoon. I was tempted to pound on his door, but I hated to wake him in the event he'd gotten in late last evening. I hadn't heard him leave after he'd dropped me at my door, but that didn't mean he hadn't simply left quietly.

Tossing the ball for Sandy one last time, I finished the last of my coffee. Having an entire day off was such an unusual occurrence that I wasn't quite sure what to do with myself. Normally, if I had a day off, I'd go surfing, hiking, or paddle boarding, none of which was an option given my current situation. Maybe a drive? Not that there was anywhere I particularly wanted to drive to, and even if there was, I couldn't drive with my feet in their current condition. If Shredder hadn't been able to track down Hoku Palakiko last night, then perhaps I'd go into the office and see what I could do to find her.

When I saw Shredder and Riptide coming in from the beach, I realized I should have known he wouldn't waste the chance to catch a few waves. I waved to the man while Sandy greeted Riptide. "How's the water?" I asked.

"Fair. The waves are pretty tame, but it's nice to just be back in the rhythm of the islands. I know I've said this before, but I've really missed this."

"And we've missed you and are happy you are home." I reached over to give Riptide a scratch behind the ears. "I know it's early, and you are trying to ease into your day, but I have to ask if you managed to track down Hoku."

Shredder frowned. "No. It seems as if both Kinsley and Hoku have disappeared without a trace. I have people working on finding them, but neither Mr. nor Mrs. Palakiko has used their phone, credit cards, or the ATM. Hoku's car is still at her estate, so it seems she left with someone else. We don't even know for certain that she was kidnapped; only that she was speaking to your dad, he was knocked out, and by the time you arrived, she was missing."

"Sounds like a kidnapping to me, which I suppose might make sense if her captor wanted to use her as leverage with her husband, but how does my being kidnapped from the Palakiko home fit into this? How did this man even know I would be there? I had no plans to visit the home prior to my mother coming by and asking me to track down my father."

"I think that was a fluke. I suspect that Tatsuo sent someone to kill or kidnap Mrs. Palakiko. I suspect that when Tatsuo's man arrived, he found your father already there, so he knocked him out. I don't know why whoever grabbed you was still there when you arrived since, Mrs. Palakiko seemed to have been gone by that point, but maybe someone was looking for something they felt Palakiko might have left in his office and you showed up before they were done."

I supposed it might have happened that way, but my gut told me there was more going on.

Chapter 12

Shredder and I sat in silence for several minutes. I suppose we were both working things through in our minds. I was about to ask Shredder about his prior run-ins with Tatsuo when my phone rang. "What's up, Jason?"

"We found Vinnie Travano's killer."

"Does that mean you found the person who killed Walter Evans and Ano Hanale as well?" I asked.

"No. I don't think so. It turns out that a man named Preston Flanders runs the nightclub that recently opened in the resort down the road from the Dolphin Bay Resort. Flanders has made millions on the mainland opening nightclubs inside casinos. He has clubs in Vegas, Reno, Atlantic City, and other gambling hubs around the country. His company recently decided to expand its enterprise to clubs contained within resorts. The resort on the North Shore is one of the first of this type, but it turns out that Flanders has plans to open clubs in Waikiki and Honolulu as well."

"Okay, I'm following so far. What does this have to do with Vinnie or with me?"

"Hang on. I'm getting there. It turns out that the management team of the Dolphin Bay Resort was approached by Flanders about opening a club where the large conference room is currently located. The Dolphin Bay Resort folks turned him down, so he moved on to the resort down the road. I guess the new nightclub is siphoning a lot of customers from Dolphin Bay, so the management team at Dolphin Bay is reconsidering their stance. A representative from Dolphin Bay approached Vinnie about opening a club on their premises. I found a contract where Vinnie had agreed to work on the logistics of such an enterprise. In addition, I found a document indicating that Vinnie was looking at a plan to partner with Dolphin Bay to approach the resorts Flanders planned to work with in Waikiki and Honolulu about contracting with them instead of Flanders in an effort to keep it local."

"So Flanders felt threatened and killed Vinnie?"

"As part of a plea deal to reduce his prison time, a man named Roland Davenport has confessed to killing Vinnie. He works for Flanders as a fixer of sorts, and has stated that he was acting on Flanders' orders when he shot and killed Vinnie Travano."

Okay, this was surprising news. "So if Davenport killed Vinnie, why involve me?"

"He didn't. At least not intentionally. It is true that the lifeguard tower where Vinnie's body was left and posed after he was shot is the tower most often used by you on Saturdays, but according to

Davenport, Vinnie's body was meant to be a message to Dolphin Bay Resort's management to reconsider their idea to get into the nightclub business and really had nothing to do with you. It just happened that Vinnie was killed on a Friday night and that you found him when you went to work on Saturday morning."

That actually made sense in terms of a motive, but it totally destroyed the theory that the murders of Evans, Travano, and Hanale were all connected. "So if Vinnie wasn't killed by the same man who killed Evans and Hanale, does that mean their murders aren't connected either?"

"I don't know. What I do know is that I need to widen my investigation. I want to pick your brain about exactly what you saw when you stumbled upon Evans' body. Can you stop by my office later this morning?"

"Yeah. I'll be there."

After I hung up, I filled Shredder in on what Jason had told me. The deepening furrows between his eyes indicated that he was as thrown by the whole thing as I was. When we were looking at a single killer for all three men, Tatsuo made sense, but if the three men were killed by different people, that theory went right out the window.

"Jason wants me to come by his office so he can pick my brain about what I may have seen or not seen on the morning I found Evans' body. You are welcome to come along if you want. It seems like it is just the two of us this weekend, so maybe we can grab lunch after."

"Yeah, I'll come. I need to grab a shower. Do you want to meet up in a half hour or so?"

"Works for me," I confirmed.

It only took me twenty minutes to shower and dress, so I used the extra ten minutes to call my dad and see how he was doing. He confirmed that he was being released later that morning and that he planned to take the weekend off to keep my mom happy. He was concerned about the whereabouts of Hoku Palakiko, but I let him know that I was working on finding her and that I would call him with updates as I received them. Dad didn't know about Shredder's superspy identity and, in fact, only knew him as my vagabond surf-chasing friend, which was too bad, since I think he would have found it comforting to know that Shredder was working on it as well.

I was just hanging up with Dad when Shredder knocked on the door. Riptide was with him, so I decided to take Sandy along as well. We could eat in an open-air restaurant since most allowed dogs, and if Jason didn't want the dogs in his office, he could come outside to talk to us.

As it turned out, Jason offered to buy us lunch if we could talk while we ate.

"I want you to walk me through the morning you found Evans' body on the beach." Jason jumped in after we'd all ordered.

"It was early. The sky was just getting light, but the sun wasn't up. I wanted to get a few runs in before I had to get ready for work, so I grabbed Sandy and my board and headed out. Sandy ran ahead of me as we approached the beach. When I arrived, Sandy was standing over the body. I checked for a pulse and then called your cell. When you didn't pick up, I called 911."

"Did you see anyone else in the area? Anyone walking on the beach? Maybe other surfers or even a boat?" Jason asked.

"No. I was the only one out and about that early."

"What did Evans have on when you found him?"

"Khaki pants and a Hawaiian shirt. Both were covered in blood, although there wasn't any visible blood on the ground. There may have been blood beneath the body, but I was asked to leave when HPD arrived, so I wasn't around to verify that one way or another."

"Did Evans have shoes on?"

"No," I answered. "His feet were bare. He did have a chain around his neck. Silver. I think he wore dog tags."

"Did you touch the body? Perhaps you looked through his pockets in order to find an ID?"

I glared at Jason. "Do you actually think I am so dumb as to touch evidence without gloves? I didn't touch anything other than the man's neck to confirm he was actually dead. I guess I knew he was dead based on his pale complexion and the blood all over his clothing, but I still felt the need to verify that he was beyond saving."

"How far from the water was the body found?" Jason asked.

"Isn't that in the report HPD filed?"

"It is. I'm just trying to help you get a visual."

I bobbed my head a bit and then responded. "I guess the body was maybe twenty feet away from the water. Perhaps a little less. It was low tide, but based on where he was lying, if it had been high tide, he would have been under water."

"Was the victim or the clothing covering the victim wet?"

"It was. We've discussed this before. In fact, we had decided that while the man could have been dumped in the water, it was just as likely he was left on the beach and got wet during high tide. Is there a reason we are going over everything again?"

"Now that we know that Vinnie wasn't intentionally left for you to find, it opens the door to the idea that none of the men were intentionally left for you to find. I just want to go over everything again."

"Okay. Go on. I'll tell you what I can."

"You said you woke up at first light. Do you remember if you heard anything? Could Sandy have heard anything? Was he restless?"

I paused as I tried to think back to that morning. "I don't remember hearing anything." I nibbled on my lower lip as I thought about it. "I do think Sandy was already up and about when I awoke. I remember considering the option of sleeping in a bit since I hadn't slept well that night, but it seemed like Sandy might need to go out, so I decided to just head down to the water and wake up that way."

"So if there had been a boat that dropped Evans on the beach, Sandy might have heard it?" Jason verified.

"Sure, if there was one, he would most likely have heard something. He's a dog. His hearing is a lot better than mine."

"And you first woke up at around five a.m.?"

"Around then, yes."

"Did you notice marks on the beach that would indicate that a boat pulled up onto the sand? The marks could have been from a motorized boat, but Evans could also have been brought ashore via a kayak, canoe, outrigger, or any number of non-motorized vessels.''

"I didn't notice. I wasn't looking for evidence of a boat, so I can't say for certain that marks weren't visible. Shouldn't that sort of thing be noted in your report?"

Jason nodded. "It was noted that no evidence of a boat was found at the scene, but as I said, I'm just going over everything again."

"Yeah, I get it. If there wasn't evidence of a boat, maybe the guy was washed up onto the beach during high tide or perhaps the guy was carried down to the beach from a vehicle. He was a big guy, but I don't suppose it would be impossible to carry him the eighth of a mile or so required to get him from the road to where I found him."

The conversation paused as our food was delivered. Shredder had been listening intently but hadn't said a word. I supposed he was honoring Jason's role as moderator for this discussion. He was, after all, the one who had wanted to talk to me.

After the server left, Jason picked up where he left off. "You said the beach was totally deserted when you arrived. You said the water was deserted as well. Is that normal for that particular beach and strip of water at sunrise on a Wednesday morning in June?"

"Yes. The waves behind the condo aren't great. Anyone who has to drive to get to a surf spot wouldn't go there, so that stretch of sea is usually only occupied by those who live close enough to walk to that location."

"There are several houses close enough in addition to the condos," Jason pointed out.

"That's true, and sometimes I run into someone, but on the morning in question I didn't."

"Okay, close your eyes and try to picture the scene that greeted you that day. Did you notice anything at all unusual or out of place?"

I did as Jason asked and closed my eyes. I tried to envision the scene that greeted me. When I came around the corner from the condos to approach the beach, I remembered seeing Sandy standing over the body. I called him back, and he came. When I arrived at the location where the body was laying, I told Sandy to stay back and then I knelt down and checked for a pulse. When I didn't find one, I called Jason and then 911. I remembered feeling fear. I remembered looking around to see if there was anyone else in the area. Perhaps the killer was lurking and watching from behind the nearby grove of trees. Once it was confirmed that the police were on the way, I got up and looked around the area. Sandy wasn't barking or growling which he would have been if someone was hiding nearby, so I was pretty sure the person who had dumped the victim on the sand, if the victim even had been dumped, was long gone.

"I'm sorry," I said. "I really don't remember seeing or hearing anything that would explain how Walter Evans came to be on the beach that morning. The idea that he might have been dumped at sea and washed up on the beach isn't a bad one. The way the tides in that area work, we have a lot of debris wash up on the beach. In fact, the gang from the condos and I try to spend at least one day a month simply picking up trash and other treasures brought to us by the tide."

"The original police report did indicate that Evans had most likely been washed up onto the beach, but then we found the body of the nightclub owner and that led us to look at the deaths as related to each other and related to you. Since Vinnie Travano died for a reason having nothing to do with you, I am going to have to consider that Evans' death might very well have been unrelated as well. If the body was placed on the beach, I would look at things much differently than I would if it randomly washed up on the beach which is why I am trying to nail down the method by which Evans ended up on the beach."

"I get it. I'm sorry, but I really don't know how the guy ended up where he did."

I glanced at Shredder. He was frowning, but he still hadn't said anything. If I had to guess, he was revisiting the theory he'd most recently settled on as well.

Chapter 13

After our lunch with Jason, Shredder and I headed back to the condo.

"I'm still trying to wrap my head around the fact that all the events we are looking might very well exist independently of the others," I said. "If that turns out to be true, then we still have three answers to find: Who killed Walter Evans, who killed Ano Hanale, and what happened to Hoku Palakiko? I suppose there is also the question of who kidnapped me and put Dad in the hospital, bringing the total questions up to four, but since I ended up in a shed on an estate owned by Tatsuo, and the man we'd been hired to find was seen with him earlier in the day, I have to assume, at the very least, that Kinsley's association with Tatsuo was related in some way to his wife's disappearance, my kidnapping, and Dad's stay in the hospital."

"I think that logic seems to fit what we know."

"In my mind, finding out what happened to Hoku Palakiko is the most urgent of the questions needing answers. I know it is likely that the woman is dead, but if there is even a slight chance she is still alive, we need to find her before it is too late."

Shredder suggested we grab cold drinks and find a place on the lanai. The area closest to the sea was located in the shade at this time of the day, so we pulled up lounge chairs, got comfortable, and settled in to brainstorm.

"We know that Kinsley Palakiko was piloting the plane that delivered Tatsuo to the airport where he met with Spade, and it has been suggested that Palakiko met Spade at a poker game that both men attended on Friday evening. So I am going to go out on a limb, and say that at some point after that Friday night game, Spade introduced Palakiko to Tatsuo. I am going to assume that Palakiko realized that flying Tatsuo around was going to make him a lot of money in a relatively short amount of time."

"That makes sense," I agreed. "But how did Hoku get wrapped up in this and what really happened on the day I was kidnapped?"

"We know Hoku hired you to find her husband. Your dad was in possession of both the knowledge that Kinsley was working for Tatsuo and a photo of the men at the airport to prove it. You've already shared that he called Hoku to deliver the news and then set up a meeting to discuss what steps she wanted him to take next. Assuming her phone was bugged, it stands to reason that Tatsuo or Spade, or someone associated with one or both of the men, could have overheard the discussion between your father and Hoku and decided to kidnap Hoku as a means of keeping her quiet about what she knew."

"If that were true, and it does make sense, why didn't they kill Dad? Why didn't they kill me? Dad and I both knew about the relationship between Tatsuo and Palakiko. It seems that if Tatsuo's intent was to keep that relationship quiet, whoever was at the house when I arrived really should have killed us both."

Shredder leaned back in his chair. He put his feet on the railing in front of him. He swatted at a fly and then took a sip of his cola. "The fact that they let you live doesn't fit what would otherwise be a pretty decent theory."

"The picture you've painted of Tatsuo makes it seem as if he is a very dangerous man who wouldn't hesitate to kill anyone who might get in his way."

"That is a factual statement."

"What about Spade? Is he as dangerous as Tatsuo?"

Shredder paused and then answered. "As we've discussed, Tatsuo has a reputation for killing anyone who gets in his way, but Spade is more of a middle man. I'm not saying he wouldn't kill, or that he hasn't already, but he doesn't have a reputation for killing without discretion."

"What if it was Spade who came to the Palakiko home on the day I was kidnapped? It actually makes more sense that it would be him, or one of his men. After all, we had seen Tatsuo fly away just hours before the incident. I have no idea where he was off to, but it seems that if he intended to stay on the island, the Dillingham Airfield was as good a place as any to transfer to ground transportation."

"So if it was Spade and not Tatsuo who is responsible for Mrs. Palakiko's disappearance, your kidnapping, and your father's injury, he may have been more likely to let you live once you and your father stumbled onto the situation."

I shrugged. "It does explain why we aren't dead. I don't know why I ended up chained to a shed on Tatsuo's property if it was Spade who kidnapped me in the first place, but I do know that the woman Spade married is actually very nice. Yes, she is the type to be impressed with money and prestige, which is probably what attracted her to Spade in the first place, but I just don't see her marrying someone who is a total creep. And then there's McCarthy."

"McCarthy?"

"He is a retired cop and a friend of Dad's. He likes to gamble and would be the sort to overlook illegal activity to a point if offered the chance to attend a private game at a luxury estate, but if Spade was the sort to kill people on a whim, I don't see McCarthy overlooking that."

"Maybe we should have a chat with this McCarthy, and see what he has to say."

I nodded. "I'll set it up."

Luckily, McCarthy was home and willing to let us stop by. Once again, Shredder drove my Jeep since I couldn't drive with my feet the way they were, and he didn't seem to have a car. McCarthy lived in a modest house in a nice neighborhood with tree-lined streets. His classic 1968 Mustang was freshly polished and in the drive. If I had to bet, he had just returned from somewhere and planned to go out again, because most of the time, he kept Jezebel in the garage where the sun couldn't fade her cherry red paint.

"Thanks for agreeing to meet with me," I said after McCarthy answered the door. "This is my friend, Shredder. He lives in the same condo complex I do."

"Happy to meet you," McCarthy shook Shredder's hand. "Have we met before?"

"I don't think so," Shredder replied.

He frowned. "Maybe not. My memory and my eyesight are going these days." He stepped aside. "Come on in. We'll head out to the lanai to chat. Can I get you some iced tea?"

Shredder and I both agreed that we'd like some.

"So how can I help you today?" McCarthy asked, after bringing out tall icy glasses.

"We wanted to ask some additional questions about Spade," I answered. I filled McCarthy in on the circumstances surrounding Spade, Tatsuo, Kinsley and Hoku Palakiko, and how we thought they might relate to my kidnapping, Dad's injury, and Hoku's disappearance. I pretty much told him everything except how Shredder fit into the whole thing. McCarthy didn't ask why I was working with the man, so I didn't offer an explanation. "I guess at this point, we want to know more about Spade. I know that you know the man casually and have been invited to play poker at his home from time to time. Does he strike you as the type to engage in illegal activity or to indiscriminately kill those who get in his way?"

"Engage in illegal activity, yes. Kill those who get in his way, no. Spade is all about the money, and he is more than willing to engage in business relationships that fall outside the boundaries set by those who govern such things. He is a big guy, and he has an intimidating way about him. I think this serves him well doing what he does. If you are asking if he would arrange for Palakiko to provide air service to Tatsuo, absolutely. But if you are asking if he would then turn around and kill the man's wife, I would have to say no. Tatsuo, on the other hand, well… that is another story."

"So if, as we suspect, Tatsuo found out that I had seen him at the airport with Spade, and that Dad knew about the meetup as well and had told Hoku, it is reasonable to suspect that Tatsuo might send Spade to clean up the mess if he was indeed somewhere other than Hawaii as we suspect?"

"Yes, that is a reasonable theory. And I suspect that Spade would oblige up to a point. I could see him detaining Palakiko's wife and possibly even using her as leverage if Palakiko began to balk at doing what he was being asked to do. I would believe a story where he knocked your father out and tied you up in a shed. He may even have turned you over to Tatsuo's men. But I very much doubt that he would have been the one to actually kill anyone. There may be a fine line between aiding in a murder and committing a murder, but it is my belief it is a line he maintains."

Okay, I suppose that explained how everything could have gone down like Shredder and I theorized. "What about Walter Evans? He was also a pilot, only he ended up dead. He seems to have been the one who was initially hired by Tatsuo to provide illegal transport. Do you think Tatsuo might have also been the one to kill him?"

"I don't think Tatsuo has spent time on the islands in quite some time. Maybe he has popped in for a meeting here and there like the one you witnessed taking place at the airport, but I'm sure he hasn't spent any more time on the island than that. I doubt he killed Evans, but he might have had him killed. The man has resources which would allow him to have pretty much anyone who got in his way killed, and he doesn't seem to have the patience for anyone who doesn't do their job."

Something occurred to me. "What do you know about a woman named Samantha Jones? She told Shredder that she was the one responsible for recruiting Evans to fly for Tatsuo. If Evans bailed on Tatsuo, do you think Jones would eliminate him if Tatsuo told her to do so?"

"Sure. I think that is very likely."

Chapter 14

Shredder and I headed to the Dolphin Bay Resort to see if we could track down Samantha Jones. Having a hunch that she was the one to have killed Evans in order to save face with Tatsuo wasn't the same as having proof. I doubted that Jones would come right out and admit it even if she had been the one to kill Evans, but Shredder wanted to try to get a better feel for the woman by following up on the conversation they'd had the previous evening. Once again, he asked me to wait for him while he went to her room, and once again, I obliged. Not only had Shredder been trained in interrogation techniques, but he was a good looking and charming guy who seemed to naturally have a way with the female portion of the population. Deciding to wait on the currently closed patio of the beachside bar, I grabbed a lounge chair and called Luke. It had been quite a while since we'd connected, and I really did want to discuss the visit he kept dangling over my head.

"Luke?" I greeted him when he answered after the first ring. "I really wasn't expecting you to answer."

"I know. I'm sorry. I know I owe you a return call and planned to make some time this morning. How are you?"

"I'm okay." I decided not to bring up all the ways I really wasn't okay. Why worry him when there was absolutely nothing he could do to help. "It's been a busy month at Pope Investigations, and I've been working a lot of hours. How are things in Texas?"

Luke paused.

"You aren't going to make it to the islands as you planned."

"I want to. I really do. I even bought airline tickets for mid-July, but my sister is expecting another baby in July, and she asked me if I would accompany the cattle from both ranches to the auction so her husband could take some time off to be with her and the baby."

"I didn't realize your sister was pregnant. Congratulations on a new niece or nephew."

"I'm sorry. I thought I told you about the baby. She is very excited, as is my brother-in-law. Anyway, it looks like I am going to have to put the trip off for another month, maybe two."

I swallowed hard. "I understand. Your family really needs you right now. How is your mom doing?"

"Not well. She is really taking my dad's death hard. I guess that is natural. They had been married for almost fifty years. I know that grief takes time, and I am doing everything I can to help her through this, but I feel totally out of my depth most of the time."

"I'm sure you are doing what you can, and it isn't all on you. You do have two sisters and two brothers."

"I know. And they do what they can. Of course, they have their own lives and their own ranches to see to. I'm not really sure what is going to happen in the long run with Dad's ranch if I don't stay. I've talked to my brothers about it, and they have a few ideas if we decide to combine herds and consolidate things."

I glanced out toward the sea. I could feel the tightness in my chest. "Do you think that is what you might do?"

"I don't know. Maybe. It's too early to tell. I don't think Mom is ready to deal with anything like that at this point, so for now, I guess I'm in a waiting game of sorts." Luke took a deep breath and blew it out. "I'm sorry this is taking so long. I wish I had a firm date for you as to when I might be back, but I don't. All I can say is that it won't be anytime soon."

A single tear rolled down my cheek. "I know. And I understand. If you are able to reschedule your visit, let me know."

"I don't suppose you want to come to Texas?"

I considered the idea. "No. Now is not a good time. Besides, you are a very busy man. The last time I was there, I barely saw you and all those cows really freaked me out. I just don't think that Texas and I are very compatible." I stood up and walked out onto the beach. I slipped off my slippers and let my feet sink into the hot sand. "I probably should go. Busy day today and all that."

"Yeah, me too. I'll try to call you tomorrow if I can. If not, the following day for sure."

I knew he wouldn't, but I still found myself saying that I looked forward to his call before I hung up and slipped my cell back into my pocket. The fact that Luke had become so entangled in his family ranch wasn't his fault. I knew that he would rather be here, but the more time that went by, the more I could see that returning to Hawaii on any sort of a permanent basis was simply not going to be in the cards for him. I thought of Kekoa in LA saying a final goodbye to Cam, and wondered if I shouldn't take a similar trip to Texas, but while Kekoa seemed ready to make that trip, I wasn't sure that I was.

I knew what was coming, and while I wouldn't have chosen any of this for Luke or me, or Luke's family for that matter, sometimes life puts up roadblocks, and the only choice is a change in direction whether the change fits with your long term plan or not. Deep in my heart, I knew that clinging to even the small shred of hope I had left would only make things harder in the long run. Maybe I should throw in the towel and end things with Luke the way Kekoa was ending things with Cam. It would be incredibly painful in the short term, but in the long run, it might make things easier on everyone.

"Everything okay?" Shredder asked after walking up behind me.

I used the back of my hand to wipe the tears from my cheek. "Everything is fine. Were you able to speak to Samantha Jones?"

"No, but I was able to let myself into her cottage. The maid was only two buildings down, so I didn't want to take a lot of time, but I found a contract between Samantha and Walter Evans which detailed the fact that he was being recruited to provide international air service for her clients between private airstrips in several cities in Asia, Honolulu, and the Main Land. We already knew this, but I also found an email from Evans letting Samantha know that he planned to terminate their contract after learning the details about the cargo he was to transport for Tatsuo. Evans wasn't specific in his email as to what the cargo he objected to consisted of, but I did find a return email to Evans from Samantha letting him know that the penalty for early termination of the contract would be severe. She persuaded Evans to meet with her to discuss the matter. It looks as if the meeting she set up was to take place here on Oahu the day before you found Evans' body on the beach. Furthermore, I found an email from Samantha to Tatsuo, letting him know that they might need to replace Evans and that she would start to look for someone with the unique qualifications they needed right away."

"Okay, everything you just told me fits the theory we've come up with. How do we use that information to prove that Samantha Jones either killed Walter Evans or had him killed and that Palakiko was hired to replace him?"

"We need to link Samantha Jones to Walter Evans' death. In her email to Evans, she mentioned a place called Devil's Door. Does that ring a bell?"

"Sure. Devil's Door is the name of a neighboring island. The island is uninhabited and rarely visited. The only reason anyone ever really goes there is because there is a deep pool in the middle of the island that is said to be so deep that the devil himself used the pool as a doorway to pass between earth and hell."

"How long would it take to go there?"

"It depends on the speed of the boat used to access the island, but if you have a decent boat, we can get there in two and a half to three hours. It'll take as long to get back, and it is already almost two o'clock now, so we might want to visit the island tomorrow when we can get an early start."

"I can arrange for a chopper. Let me make a call. If the island is three hours away by boat, we should be able to get there in a fraction of the time by air."

I waited while Shredder stepped away and made a call. He hung up and then called someone else. After the second call he made was complete, he returned to my side, took my hand, and headed toward the parking lot.

"So did you get a chopper?"

"I did. The pilot's name is Dawson. Don't ask a lot of questions about how we know each other. He won't be able to answer you, and it might create an awkward situation since Dawson is the friendly sort who won't be comfortable with a lie."

"Got it. Dawson is one of your spy buddies."

Shredder shot me a lopsided grin which seemed to indicate that I didn't know the half of it.

As Shredder had indicated he would be, Dawson was a friendly guy who had lived and worked on the islands for over twenty years. He'd been to Devil's Door before and seemed to know exactly where to land. He offered to wait for us while Shredder and I had a look around. Shredder promised to be back within two hours, so Dawson found a shady spot and settled in for a nap.

Devil's Door was a small island. Mostly round in shape, it was only a few miles or so across and was mostly barren. A deep pool of salt water was near the middle of the island. I supposed the only explanation was that the land mass was shaped like a donut with a hole in the center which opened up to the sea.

Shredder began to walk slowly away from the site where Dawson had landed the chopper. He seemed to be looking for something. Perhaps footprints? A good wind or rain would most likely have destroyed any prints that would have existed more than three weeks ago, but I supposed that if you wanted to find a clue as to what might have gone on, looking down at the ground was probably our best option.

After looking around for less than twenty minutes, Shredder held up a hand and stopped walking.

"Did you find something?" I asked.

"Blood. A lot of it."

Shredder took the small daypack he wore off. He took out a pair of gloves and a baggie and began gathering leaves from the ground which were covered with dry blood.

"I guess if we can match the DNA from the blood to Evans' DNA, we'll have that piece of the puzzle solved at least." I looked around. "I wonder why Samantha had Evans come all the way out here."

"I don't know, and at this point, we don't know this blood even belonged to Evans. For all we know, the blood could even have come from an animal." Shredder pointed. "Let's head over there."

Forty minutes later, Shredder and I found a small wooden building which looked to be built into the side of the cliff that occupied the northern end of the island. At first, the building appeared to be abandoned, but once we got closer, we were able to see that a heavily armed man wearing fatigues was standing near the entrance.

"What could possibly be in that shed that would warrant an armed guard in this remote location?" I asked Shredder.

"I don't know, but the chances are the man with the gun saw us land and has most likely alerted whomever he checks in with." Shredder looked around. "We should probably go. We can return by boat after dark. If we approach on the far side of the island, we can probably take a look around without anyone knowing we're here."

"Okay. That sounds like a good plan."

Shredder and I hurried back to the chopper since we really had no idea what sort of backup the man at the shed might have called for, and at this point, we had exactly zero weapons. Dawson wasn't happy about being woken up from his nap, but after we explained the urgency of taking off before reinforcements arrived, he quickly sprang into action. Once we arrived back on Oahu, Shredder arranged for a boat, and I arranged for Brody to dogsit Sandy and Riptide overnight. Of course, that brought up questions as to where Shredder and I were going that would require overnight dog care, but I simply told him that Shredder was helping me with one of the cases Pope Investigations was working on and left it at that. I considered letting Jason know where we were going, but he'd probably forbid me from going, so I decided not to.

Chapter 15

We timed it to arrive at Devil's Door just as the darkness of night set in. Shredder anchored offshore, and we used a dinghy to row in. Once we arrived on the beach, we set off toward the opposite side of the island where we'd seen the small structure earlier in the day. I noticed that Shredder wore a much larger pack on his back tonight than he'd worn earlier in the day and wondered what sort of supplies he might have thought to bring. Shredder wanted to avoid using flashlights while we were out in the open, and luckily, it was a clear night, so we were able to navigate by the light of the moon alone.

I heard a rustling in the tall grass but decided it must be the wind. The island had no fresh water, so it wasn't home to any animals. We walked briskly so we would have the time we needed to assess the situation and then come up with a plan. By the time we made our way around to the small structure, it was completely dark. The structure, like the surrounding landscape, was dark as well. I didn't suppose the structure had power unless it was sun or wind generated.

"So, what now?" I asked Shredder as we stopped behind a small dune, and he studied the structure with his binoculars.

"We need to get closer. I don't see anyone, but that doesn't mean there isn't anyone around. We'll need to move quietly, and stay in the shadows as much as is possible."

I looked around at the barren landscape. "There isn't a lot to hide behind."

"True, but the structure is built into the side of the cliff, so I'm going to suggest we approach from behind. We'll need to circle back and then come inland."

I nodded. "Lead the way, and I'll keep up."

Shredder looked down at my feet. "No. I want you to wait here. You've been a real trooper today, but I have a feeling you must be in a lot of pain by now." He handed me a pair of binoculars and a handheld radio. "The radio is a short-range radio which is on a closed frequency that only we can hear. I want you to keep an eye on the front of the building. Let me know if you see any sign of life."

I really hated being left behind, but my feet were throbbing by this point, so I nodded and then verbally agreed to the plan. I felt a moment of panic as Shredder disappeared from the site, but then I reminded myself that no one knew we were here and I'd be fine as long as I stayed silent and out of sight.

Waiting was boring. After thirty minutes, I found myself wishing there was someone lurking around who I could watch. Of course, things would go a lot smoother if the man who had been on the island earlier had left, but smoother and exciting were usually on opposite sides of the coin.

After sixty minutes passed, I heard Shredder's voice over the radio. "I'm in position. Do you see anything?"

I was about to answer no when I noticed a figure approaching the small structure from the opposite end of the beach where we'd landed. "Yes. There is someone. A single individual. Male, I think. He is carrying a canvas bag."

"What is he doing?"

"He's approaching the structure." I swallowed hard. "Now, he is opening the door. He went inside."

"Damn."

"Maybe he is just checking on things. Maybe he will leave soon."

"Keep an eye on the building. I'll stay where I am for a few minutes."

After about five minutes, the man came out of the building with two other people. Both women. The man and the women he now had with him headed toward the beach. I radioed Shredder to tell him what was going on.

"Okay, I'm going to head in the direction of the beach. I want to see where they are going."

"I'm closer to the beach. I'll take a look," I said. "You check the shed before he comes back."

With that, I turned and hurried back toward the beach where we'd landed earlier in the day. I tried to stay low so as not to be seen. The man I was following seemed focused on the women, so I sort of doubted he'd notice me anyway. Once I arrived at the last little set of dunes before the beach flattened out, I squatted down and focused the binoculars Shredder had given me. The man shoved the two women into a rubber raft and then rowed out to a larger boat. There was another man on the boat who helped the two women onto the deck, and then the man in the raft started back toward the shore while the man in the larger boat took off with the women.

I quietly shared what I'd seen with Shredder.

"There are five women in a cell in the shed," Shredder said. "I'm going to get them out and then head toward the dinghy. You need to make your way to the dinghy as quickly as possible."

"The man with the raft is coming back."

"We'll need a distraction." Shredder paused. "Okay, come back to the structure. Get here as quickly as you can."

"On my way." I took off at a run in spite of the fact that each step resulted in a bolt of pain up my leg. I got back to the shed just as the man in the raft was pulling it up onto the beach. Shredder was waiting with the five women, who he'd managed to free. He said something to them in a language I didn't understand and then he looked at me.

"Get these women to the dinghy as quickly as you can. I'll meet you there. If I don't make it back to the dinghy by the time our friend from the raft shows up, leave, and get them to the boat."

"But..."

"Just do it. Now go. And hurry."

With that, I nodded at the women and waved for them to follow me. They hesitated, but Shredder said something in their language and they started after me. They were thin and looked to be barely able to walk, let alone run. I just hoped they'd keep up and I hoped

Shredder would do whatever it was he was going to do and meet me by the time we arrived at the dinghy.

The women were obviously terrified, but they managed to keep up with me better than I expected. Of course, with my feet in the state they were in, I wasn't exactly moving along at my top speed. When we were maybe halfway between the structure where the women had been detained, and the dinghy, a huge explosion pierced the night sky. The explosion came from the general location of the structure, although if I had to guess, it most likely originated behind the little dunes where Shredder had been hiding. Saying a silent prayer that he was okay and on his way to meet us, I picked up the pace just a bit.

We arrived at the dinghy before Shredder, so as instructed, I loaded the women and headed out to where the boat was anchored. When we arrived at the boat, I helped the women aboard and then turned to look a back toward the beach. Shredder had just arrived. I was about to go back for him, but he plunged into the sea and started swimming toward the boat. I started the engine and began to reel in the anchor. I wasn't going to leave Shredder, but I figured it would be a good idea to be ready once he reached us. Shredder was about fifty feet from the boat when the first shot was fired.

"Swim faster!" I yelled.

"Toss me a line and go."

I tossed a long rope that was attached to the deck into the water. Shredder grabbed it, and I moved the throttle to head slowly out to sea. When I saw a splash in the water just next to Shredder's head and realized it was a bullet, I upped the speed just a bit. Once I was sure we were out of gunshot range, I stopped the boat and lowered the stairs for Shredder to climb in.

"That was close," I said after giving him a hard wet hug as he climbed onto the deck.

"Too close. Let's get out of here."

Chapter 16

Saturday, June 29

By the time Shredder and I made it back to Oahu and turned the women we'd rescued over to Jason, it was the wee hours of the morning. Jason still needed to get an official statement, so we waited around to speak to him. By the time I finally made it back to my condo, the sun had risen. I knew I should be exhausted, but for some reason, I felt stimulated. Overly stimulated. The odds were that I would crash and burn at some point, but for now, I chose to sit out on the lanai, sip my cup of coffee, and soak my feet in a medicated bath. Shredder was salty from his swim out to the boat, so he'd headed toward his condo to take a shower.

I leaned my head back against the cushion I was sitting on and thought about the past few hours. Once we were underway, Shredder had shared that the small building we'd seen contained a cell which was carved into the cliff behind the building and secured with bars. The women were in the cell, and the only other thing in the room was a small sitting area for whoever might be on guard duty. Shredder knew enough Chinese to communicate with the women, who shared with him the story of being taken from the streets of Hong Kong, temporarily hidden in an old warehouse, and then transported by plane to an airfield where they were met by a utility truck which took them to a boat which brought them to the island where they were imprisoned. In the beginning, there were more than twenty of them, but every few days someone would come by and take two or three of the women. Once the women were taken, those left behind never saw them again. They didn't know if the women had been killed or moved or what.

One woman recognized a photo of Walter Evans as the man who piloted the plane that brought them to Hawaii. None of the women recognized Tatsuo, but that didn't mean he wasn't behind the whole thing. The women reported that they had been taken care of, at least to a degree. They were supplied with plenty of bottled water and given food twice a day. The guard took them out in pairs and let them walk around and see to nature's call in the morning, afternoon, and then again just before dark.

The women hadn't been injured or tortured, yet understandably, they were terrified. Once they'd supplied HPD and the FBI with the information they desired, they'd been assured that they'd be returned home to their families. While the women had provided a definite link between the men who kidnapped them and Evans, they could not provide a link between Evans and Tatsuo. Shredder had paperwork that showed a link between Evans and Samantha Jones and between Samantha Jones and Tatsuo, so in his opinion, an arrest warrant for Tatsuo would eventually be issued. Of course, Tatsuo was a slippery one, so a warrant by no means guaranteed an arrest, although it would allow them to get a warrant to search any property on the island owned by Tatsuo.

"Are you still awake?" I heard Shredder ask.

I opened my eyes. "I'm awake. Just trying to relax." I sat up a bit straighter. "You look refreshed."

"I feel refreshed. How are your feet?"

I shrugged. "Been better. Been worse. I guess I should have brought a towel and fresh bandages out with me."

"Hang on. I'll get them."

Shredder ran into my condo and then came back a minute later with the supplies I'd need. I reached for them. "Let me," he said, pulling a chair up next to me and gently picking up one of my feet and putting it on the towel he had draped across his lap. I wanted to cry with gratitude when he gently began to pat it dry.

"So, what now?" I asked. "We saved the women who were still on the island, which I am very happy about, although I wish we could have saved the others as well. Still, five is better than none. But other than the fact we saved these women, are we really any closer to finding Kinsley and Hoku Palakiko, or capturing Tatsuo and bringing him to justice?"

"No, I'm afraid we aren't."

"And did we learn anything new about either Walter Evans' death or Ano Hanale's? I suppose, given the blood we found earlier, we can speculate that Evans was shot on the island, brought to the beach behind the condo, and left for me to find."

Shredder began wrapping the foot he'd just dried. "Actually, we don't know that. The blood we found is not a match for Evans. In fact, it came from a female. I would assume one of the women who decided not to cooperate.'

I cringed. The very thought of what those women had gone through made me sick.

"I know it seems like we aren't getting anywhere, but we are," Shredder assured me. "These sorts of things take time. They take patience."

"I've never been big on patience."

Shredder gently slipped one of the open-air shoes on my foot that he'd just bandaged, picked up the other one, and began to dry it as he had the first one. "I've been trying to nail Tatsuo down for years. I've been actively tracking him for months. I'll get him. Eventually. I don't know where and I don't know when, but I'll get him."

"So what do I do in the meantime? Just sit here waiting for something to happen even though we have no idea whether or not the Palakikos are dead or alive. And if they are alive, are they with Tatsuo voluntarily, or are they being held against their wills?"

"Jason is working on a warrant to search Tatsuo's estate. I don't know if we will find our answers there, but we might. In the meantime, how about breakfast? My treat."

"Breakfast sounds good. I'm starving," I said as he began wrapping my other foot. "Maybe a big Loco Moco."

"I haven't had one of those in months." Shredder slipped my wrapped foot into my clunky shoe. "Just let me grab my wallet. After we eat, we can swing by Luke's place and pick up the dogs."

I knew that it was Brody and not Luke who had taken care of the dogs, but just hearing Shredder say *Luke's place* brought a painful tightness to my chest.

******

Surprisingly, the best Loco Mocos on the island could be found at a food truck parked down by the beach. Deciding to buy the calorie heavy feasts from the food truck and then eat at one of the picnic tables provided, we headed down the highway toward our destination. Shredder instructed me to find a table while he stood in line for our food. I found a nice table in the shade that overlooked the sea and sat down before someone else claimed it. While I sat there waiting, I looked out over the Saturday morning crowd that was beginning to congregate on the water and wondered about Ano. It had turned out that Vinnie's death was not related to Tatsuo, and Evans seemed more likely than not to be directly correlated to his relationship with the guy, but where did Ano fit into this whole thing? He had been deposited in a location where I would find him, so initially, I assumed he'd been shot by the same killer as the others, but with the new information we had, I realized that was not the case. In fact, on most any other morning, it would have been Dad who found the body since nine times out of ten, he showed up to work before I did. He'd gone to the South Shore on that particular morning, so I'd arrived first. Perhaps

Ano hadn't been placed there to gain my attention as I'd suspected he had.

Had the killer been trying to gain Dad's attention rather than mine? Was Ano's death somehow related to one of the cases we were working on and was his murder a message of some sort? I supposed it would be worthwhile to take a second look at the situation.

"Oh, wow. Those are even bigger than I remembered," I said as Shredder put my plate in front of me.

"Just eat what you can. They look delicious, but I doubt I'll finish mine either."

I took a large bite of the gravy covered beef patty over rice and chewed slowly. Heaven. "I've been thinking about Ano Hanale," I said after I swallowed. "Given the fact that it appeared at the time that Evans, Travano, and Hanale had all been left for me to find, I assumed all three deaths were related. Now it looks as if the three deaths aren't related. We know who killed Vinnie and it wasn't Tatsuo, and we never really did find a link between Ano and the other victims or Ano and Tatsuo, so maybe his death has nothing to do with the others."

"Do you have a theory?"

I took another bite and chewed slowly. I washed it down with a sip of the water Shredder had bought. "I'm not sure. Ano's body was left just inside the front door of Pope Investigations. At the time, I believed the man was left for me to find, as I'd believed the others had been, but when I really stopped to think about it, I realized that it is my dad and not me, who almost always arrives at work first. The only reason he hadn't on that particular day was because he had a meeting on the South Shore that morning and went there directly from home."

"Okay, so say the body was left for your dad, or maybe it was left as a message for the firm overall. Has Pope Investigations taken on any cases relating to Hanale or to food trucks in general?"

"No. Not really." I paused to think about it. "There was this one case that involved a man who owned a restaurant on the North Shore who was trying to get the food trucks in the area near his restaurant moved."

"Sounds like a familiar conflict."

"It is, and while both the restaurant owner and the food trucks which were affected were very passionate about their stance, I don't think the conflict was the sort of thing to lead to murder."

"I'm afraid it doesn't take a lot to drive someone to murder," Shredder pointed out. "So, what happened? Did the trucks have to move?"

"No. It was decided that they were legally parked and were working from legally obtained permits. The food trucks had been in the area well before the man who wanted them moved had purchased the restaurant. Basically, the restaurant owner was told to play nice, or he would be the one to be shut down."

Shredder's lips twitched just a bit. "I bet he wasn't happy about that."

"He wasn't, but the reality is that if he had a problem with food trucks, he should have checked out the regulations in the area before buying the restaurant. As you know, food trucks are an important part of our culture here on the island, and they aren't going away any time soon."

Shredder downed a third of his water and then continued the conversation. "Okay, assuming that it wasn't the restaurant owner who killed Ano and literally left him on your doorstep, any other guesses?"

"Not really."

"Any other cases that involved food trucks or food truck owners, even if the food truck link is more of an adjacent link and not a direct link?"

I frowned. "What do you mean?"

"Maybe a food truck was involved in an auto accident, or one of the food truck owners was involved in a bar fight. If something like that happened, but the victim didn't know the identity of the person involved, they might target food trucks in general as a means of tracking the guy down."

"There was a case that Dad turned down where a man wanted to hire us to prove that one of the food trucks, he didn't know which one, was being used to distribute fake ID's to high school students."

"Why did your dad turn down the case?"

"The guy didn't seem to have his facts straight. In fact, Dad said the guy really didn't have any facts, only speculation. I guess the guy caught his daughter with a fake ID, and when questioned, she told him that she had bought the ID from a food truck, but she didn't remember which one. When my dad told the man he would look into it but that he needed a few days to finish up another case before he could give much time to the situation, the man went ballistic. In the end, Dad kicked him out."

"So theoretically the father of this girl with the fake ID could have tracked Ano down on his own, killed him, and then left him for your dad as a sort of *I told you so*."

"Theoretically, I suppose it could have happened that way, but that would be insane. I mean do you really think some guy would kill the man who sold a fake ID to his daughter?"

Shredder shrugged. "What do you know about the guy who tried to hire you?"

"Nothing. Dad spoke to him, I didn't."

"But there would be a file of some sort back in the office."

"Sure, I guess."

"Maybe we should go and take a look after we eat."

I raised a brow. "Really. The idea that some guy would kill Ano just because he sold a fake ID to his daughter is pretty out there. Digging into his backstory seems like a waste of time."

"You said that the man went ballistic when your dad couldn't work on his case right away. Does that seem like a normal response?"

"No," I admitted. "In fact, Dad and I both agreed that the man was wacko. I guess it wouldn't hurt to dig up the file."

Chapter 17

There was still crime scene tape across the front door of Pope Investigations, so Shredder and I headed around to the back. I used my key to let us in and then headed directly toward Dad's office. I supposed I'd need to call Jason and ask him how long it would be before we could reopen for business. Based on the fact the tape was still present today, it wouldn't Monday and probably not even Tuesday.

"So how is it working with your dad?" Shredder asked as I dug through the file cabinet looking for the file relating to Rex Harkins.

"It's been really great. So great. Having a macho cop for a dad and having five macho brothers all planning to join the force when they got old enough, left me feeling left out. I suppose part of the reason I was so determined to become a cop was to fit in and become one of the team. Of course, neither my father nor any of my brothers supported me in my campaign to reach that goal, and it really hurt. Everyone, including my father, seemed to think I was my mother's daughter, and just a frilly and helpless little thing that needed to be coddled and protected. I love my mother, but to be honest, for most of my life, there was nothing I wanted more than recognition from my father. Then Jason was shot, which was awful for everyone, and my other four brothers totally shut my dad out of the investigation, which was bad for Dad, but good for me, because when I suggested the two of us should work together, he said yes. We saved the day and solved the case, and I believe that for the first time in my life, he saw me as a real person. Suddenly I was the strong, capable woman who saved his life, and not just Mom's daughter. It was truly the proudest moment of my life in spite of the fact I missed my chance at the academy due to a broken arm." I pulled out a file. "Found it."

Shredder opened the file and studied the basic information sheet. Then, he took out his phone and made a call. "Hello, love. It's Shredder. I need a favor."

I watched while he listened.

"No, not that kind of favor. I need you to find everything you can on a man named Rex Harkins." Then, he recited Rex's address, phone number, and driver's license number. He thanked whoever was on the other end and hung up. He looked at me. "We should have something in a few minutes. In the meantime, let's see what your dad said about the man."

"As I've already shared, Mr. Harkins had come to Pope Investigations to hire us to track down the food truck vendor his daughter had told him she had purchased a fake ID from. When my dad asked why he didn't go to the police, he said he had, but he could see that they weren't going to put a lot of effort into finding the guy. When my dad said he would need a few days to finish up another case before he could give much time to the situation, the man went ballistic, and Dad kicked him out. Dad noted that the man was wound up and agitated, and seemed to be looking for a fight from the minute he arrived at our office. He understood that someone selling fake ID's to teens was not a matter to take lightly, but he also didn't understand why the man was as upset as he had been. Dad made a note to dig into the man's past if he ever returned, but he hadn't, so Dad moved on."

"This says that the man was married with three children," Shredder said. "Do we know which of the three purchased the ID?"

I looked through the notes on the sheet I was looking at. "Hillary. She was just sixteen but was able to obtain a license stating that she was twenty-two." I held up a photo. "With the right hair and makeup, I'm sure she was able to pass as twenty-two with no problem."

Shredder's phone rang. He answered. "So what did you find?"

He listened. His face grew grim. "Okay, love. Thanks. I owe you one." He hung up and looked at me. "Hillary had a sister, Hannah. A drunk driver ran Hannah down when she was seven. She died at the scene of the accident. The driver was a sixteen-year-old girl with a fake ID who had been out drinking on the day of the accident."

My hand flew to my mouth. "Oh, god. No wonder the guy was so outraged when he found his daughter's fake ID. The whole thing makes a lot more sense now."

"It does," Shredder agreed. "This man could very well have been seriously crazed after finding out that Hillary was traveling down the same path as Hannah's killer. I know it seems like a stretch, but I suppose he experienced a sense of urgency that wasn't really warranted. When he went to the police, and they didn't demonstrate the amount of urgency he expected, he went to your father. When your dad likewise wasn't as up in arms as the man expected him to be, I suspect he went after the ID dealer on his own."

"Ano."

"That would be my guess."

"I guess we need to have another chat with Ano's cousin, Keo."

Shredder and I replaced the file and straightened up the office to erase the fact that we'd been there. We locked up and then headed to the beach where we found Keo selling fish tacos. We pulled him aside and asked about the fake ID's. Initially, he didn't admit that Ano was selling them, but after we provided the reason why we needed to know, he came clean and said that yes, Ano had been selling fake ID's to underage customers, and yes, a man with a chip on his shoulder had come by on the day before he died looking to confront him about it. I figured it was time to turn the whole thing over to Jason, so I called him and filled him in and then went home and slept straight through until the following morning.

Chapter 18

Sunday, June 30

When I awoke the following morning, Sandy was staring at me. I guess Shredder must have gone and picked up the dogs from Brody at some point. I felt bad that I'd forgotten about my best buddy, but, as I predicted I would, after talking to Jason, I totally crashed. In fact, I think I fell asleep on the way home. Shredder must have carried me to bed. The twenty-four hours prior to my long nap had been hectic, to say the least. Not only had we rescued five women from an uncertain future but it also looked like we had managed to solve Ano Hanale's murder, although I supposed it would be up to Jason to get a confession or find the proof we needed.

Not being quite ready to roll out of bed, I called Sandy up onto the bed and curled up next to his comforting body. I knew Kekoa was still in LA so I supposed if I allowed myself to lounge a bit, no one would be any the wiser. Besides, it was Sunday. Wasn't lounging what Sundays were for? I was trying to decide between going back to sleep and having coffee on the lanai when my phone buzzed. It was Jason.

"What's up, big bro?"

"Thanks to the work you and Shredder did in the past couple of days, I was able to get a warrant to search Tatsuo's estate. I won't go so far as to say we found a smoking gun, but we did find a document pertaining to a storage unit near Halawa Heights. After a bit of finagling, we managed to get a warrant to open the storage unit where we found files on the women he'd kidnapped and smuggled out of China. I wish I could say that the documents we found would help us track these women down, but it will be an uphill battle to do so. We did find information relating to many of the men the women were allegedly sold to, so we are following up on that, but my feeling, at this point, is that the men were dealers and the women are long gone."

I blew out a breath. "Well, that's depressing. Did you find a lead that will help us find Kinsley and Hoku Palakiko?"

Jason hesitated. My heart began to pound.

"They're dead, aren't they?"

"I'm afraid Mr. Palakiko is. We found his remains in a shallow grave on the estate."

"And Mrs. Palakiko?"

"We still don't know what happened to her, but I would guess she is dead as well."

"So you think Tatsuo or his men killed his pilot?"

"The evidence would suggest as much."

I sat up straighter. "But that makes no sense. Why would a very intelligent and street smart man like Tatsuo kill someone whom everyone is looking for and then dump him in a shallow grave on his own property?"

"I don't know. I had the same thought, but we found what we found. I wondered something similar when you were imprisoned in the shed on the estate linking your kidnapping directly to Tatsuo. That didn't make sense either."

"Shredder said that Tatsuo hasn't been on the island for months other than his brief stopovers such as the one we witnessed at the airfield. Maybe someone other than Tatsuo is acting on his behalf. Maybe this person is sloppy."

"Maybe or maybe someone is intentionally trying to focus our attention on Tatsuo."

I supposed Jason made a good point. Maybe someone other than Tatsuo kidnapped me, killed Kinsley, and then left evidence to be easily found to pin everything on a man who might not even be involved. "Did you find a link to Spade?"

"No, and I was unable to get a warrant to search Spade's home since I didn't have a single thing to link Spade to Tatsuo other than the fact that you observed him meeting with Tatsuo at the airstrip. Apparently, that wasn't enough. I did dig around and found out that Spade is on the mainland and is not due to return to Oahu until mid-week. It occurred to me that perhaps you could score an invite to his place via your friendship with his wife. If you wanted to take a look around while you were there, I wouldn't be upset by that."

"Are you seriously asking for my help rather than lecturing me to stay out of it?"

"I'm as surprised as you are, but yes, that is exactly what I am doing. You would be wired so we could keep track of you and backup would be nearby. Maybe you can use Jasmine's relationship with Luke as an excuse to meet. Maybe she left something at Luke's place, or you wanted to ask her about some sort of a party for Luke once he finally returns or something along those lines."

Just the suggestion of a party for Luke's return made me want to pull the covers over my head and escape reality for a while longer, but I found myself agreeing to try.

"Remember, even though Spade is not on the premises, you know he will have men keeping an eye on things. You'll need to be careful."

"I will." I glanced out the window. "Jason, do you think it is possible that Spade isn't linked to the human trafficking thing?"

"Possible, yes. Likely, no."

"I want to shut the operation down, and I want to do it sooner rather than later, but if Spade is guilty, I feel bad for Jasmine. She actually is a very nice woman."

"I know. I feel bad for her as well, but if she is married to a man who is wrapped up with a man who kidnaps other men's wives, sisters, and daughters, don't you think she deserves to know that?"

"I do. I'll call Jasmine, and let you know how it goes."

A call to Jasmine to discuss a welcome home party for Luke netted me the results I was after, and she invited me to stop by. I felt bad that I'd had to lie to the woman. She was Luke's friend, and here I was getting her hopes up that Luke was going to be coming back to the islands when I knew he probably wasn't. I supposed once all this was over, I could apologize and explain things. Since Jasmine wasn't able to meet until later that afternoon, I grabbed a cup of coffee and headed out onto the lanai. Shortly after I settled in, Shredder joined me. After the normal greetings, I filled him in on my conversation with Jason.

"I'm sorry to hear about Palakiko, but I have to admit I'm not surprised. When Mrs. Palakiko was taken and neither the husband nor wife showed up again, I pretty much assumed that we'd eventually find them dead."

I tucked my legs up under my body. "I know; me too. I suppose technically, Mrs. Palakiko hasn't been found, but I imagine it is only a matter of time until she is. I hate that so many people are being hurt because of one man's greed."

"I think it comes down to the greed of many men, but I agree with you." Shredder took a sip of his coffee. "I've been thinking about the discussion you had with Jason relating to the unlikelihood that Tatsuo would bury Palakiko on his estate. I have to agree that makes little sense, and my experience with those who work for men like Tatsuo, indicates they aren't generally free thinkers. They tend to do what they are told."

"So, what are you saying?"

"I'm saying that it is likely that it was someone whose intent it is to finger Tatsuo. Someone who both kidnapped you and left you tied up on the estate, and killed and buried Palakiko on the estate."

"Finger Tatsuo? For what? We know he is guilty? Right?"

"We know or at least have strong reason to believe he is the person behind the human trafficking, but we really have not been able to link him to your kidnapping, the death of Walter Evans, or the death of Kinsley Palakiko. Remember, as far as we know, he hasn't even been on the island. Now, it could have been that one of his men acted on his own, but I really doubt it. For one thing, there aren't many of Tatsuo's men around. In fact, I have only been able to identify one guard, the caretaker, and the caretaker's wife as even being on the property."

"So who has been doing the killing?"

"Exactly. My guess at this point is that someone who wants to draw attention to Tatsuo is behind the deaths. Things have been handled much too sloppily for any of this to have been orchestrated at Tatsuo's hand."

I leaned forward and rested my elbows on my thighs. "Okay, then who?"

"At first, I thought it might be Spade. I figured he might not want Tatsuo getting a foothold of any sort on the island that he seems to consider his territory. But now, I'm not so sure. I suppose it could be Spade. The men did meet, but we don't know why they met. They may have met to discuss a conflict between the two of them having to do with territory. But the meeting they had had a much more casual feel to it. I didn't pick up the completion vibe."

"Yeah. They weren't yelling or anything."

"And they were each accompanied by only one other man. It all looked very tame and cordial."

"So if not Spade, then who?" I asked.

Shredder didn't answer. He narrowed his gaze and took another sip of his coffee. It appeared he was noodling on the idea and would most likely come up with an answer in his own time. I'd watched him work through an issue in the past and, while it might take him some time to get the answer he was after, he usually always did. Eventually, he spoke. "The only missing key at this point seems to be Samantha Jones. We know she was involved with finding both Walter Evans and Kinsley Palakiko to pilot the planes used by Tatsuo. We don't know for certain that she has killed anyone, but as the person who recommended these pilots to Tatsuo, it seems as if she would have a vested interest in how they performed. Apparently, based on the fact that both are dead, we have to assume they didn't do all that well."

"Do you think she killed these men or had them killed because she put her reputation on the line?"

"Maybe. Although there does seem to be more going on than just that. Maybe Samantha Jones isn't voluntarily working for Tatsuo. What if she is being forced to work for him in order to pay off a debt or something similar? It's possible she wants to fulfill her obligation and maybe find a way to get Tatsuo off her back if her debt to him is excessive."

"It's a good theory. How do we prove it?"

He looked at his watch. "I don't know, but you have your meeting with Jasmine. Go ahead and get ready, and I'll do the same. I'm coming along to keep an eye on things. From a distance, of course. After you meet with her, we'll talk some more about Samantha Jones. Maybe I will have had the chance to come up with something by then.

Chapter 19

Jasmine had instructed me to ring the bell when I arrived at the estate, and that someone would meet me at the gate and escort me inside. I had to admit I felt somewhat intimidated by the whole thing, but I did as I was told. The man who met me at the gate was a large man with a revolver strapped to his leg. He was a taciturn sort who never expressed a single facial expression as he asked for my ID, which I presented. Once he was satisfied that I was who I proclaimed to be, he escorted me to the patio area at the rear of the house. Jasmine was waiting for me at a poolside table. When she saw me, she stood up and offered me a hug.

"I was so happy to get your call," she said. "I was sure that Luke was gone for good."

"Yes, it did seem that way. He's been away for a long time, so I figured that getting everyone together once he returns would be a good idea. I'm really just in the initial stages of planning, but I wanted to get your input."

"I see." Jasmine poured me a tall glass of sweet tea. "And when exactly will he be returning?"

I hesitated.

"He's not really coming home is he?"

I still didn't answer.

"You are a terrible liar, Lani Pope. Why is it that you are really here?"

"Honestly, I'm here because I have reason to believe that Spade is working with a man named Mikayo Tatsuo to smuggle kidnapped women into the country."

Jasmine frowned at me. "So you are just using me to get to Spade. I should have known. I'm afraid you've wasted your time. Spade isn't here."

I took a sip of my tea. "I know. I actually hoped to have a chance to look around."

Jasmine narrowed her gaze. "Look around? Why?"

I glanced behind me to make sure we weren't being observed and then answered. "I have reason to believe that Spade helped to broker a relationship between Tatsuo and a man named Kinsley Palakiko. I actually saw the three men together several days ago, and I know Spade invited Palakiko to his Saturday night poker game. The man has since been found dead."

"And you think Spade killed him?"

"It is one of many theories."

Jasmine folded her hands on the table. "I will admit that not everything Spade does is legal, and if I'd known the extent of his operations from the start, I would never have married him, but Spade is not a killer. I know he isn't necessarily one of the good guys, but of all the questionable things he does, I don't believe killing this man would be one of them."

"If Spade didn't kill Palakiko, do you know what role he played in the relationship between Palakiko and Tatsuo?"

Jasmine looked around and then answered, lowering her voice as if she too was afraid of being overheard. "Spade does not discuss his business dealings with me, but I do lurk, and I will admit that I have overheard things Spade probably doesn't know I've overheard."

"Such as?"

"A few days ago, he was speaking to someone on the phone. I'm not certain who was on the other end, although I do have my suspicions. It seems that the person Spade was speaking to needed leverage to get someone else to do what they wanted, so the person on the phone hoped Spade would lend a hand."

"Lend a hand how? Does he rough people up for a living?"

"No, he blackmails, hustles, or bribes them. He has several ways of doing this, depending on the individual and their weakness."

I paused to consider this. "So theoretically, he might arrange for someone to win big at poker, thereby getting their confidence up, and then he might invite them to a private game at his home on the following evening. He would make sure the target not only lost but lost big. He might even persuade the target to borrow money to continue in the hope of getting even, thereby putting the target in his debt?"

Jasmine looked at me with suspicion in her eyes. "I'd say that is one of the stings he has executed in the past. You seem to know more than you are letting on."

"Not really. I'm just trying to take the facts I have and make them fit. Have you ever heard of a woman named Samantha Jones?"

Jasmine's eyes narrowed. "Is she wrapped up in this?"

I nodded. "Yes. I'm just trying to figure out to what extent she is involved."

"I knew it. Spade said I shouldn't worry about her, but I knew they'd been seeing each other again."

"Again?" I asked.

"Spade and Samantha used to date. Actually, that isn't accurate. What they used to do was have sex. A lot of it from what I've been led to understand. After Spade and I got together, I asked about his relationship with Samantha, and he said it was over. I chose to believe him, but recently I've begun to suspect that she is back in the picture. I've overheard him speaking to her on the phone on several occasions, and Ace mentioned her in passing."

"Ace?"

"Spade's right-hand man." Jasmine wiped a tear from her eye. "Darn it."

"I'm sorry to have to bring up such a painful topic."

Jasmine took a deep breath and offered me a glance. "Don't be. It's my own fault. I should have known that getting involved with someone like Spade was a bad idea. I really do love him, and I believe he loves me, but I honestly doubt he'll ever be done with her."

"If Samantha has done what I have reason to believe she has done and I can prove it, she will be spending a good long time in prison."

"Well, I guess that's something." Jasmine adjusted her position and looked me in the eye. "How can I help?"

"Samantha has admitted to acting as a headhunter for Tatsuo and others involved in illegal activities, and we suspect she may be responsible for at least two deaths. The problem is that we can't prove any of this. We know that Spade and Tatsuo have been working together, and I am hoping that if I can take a look around, I will be able to find something to prove what we think we've already figured out."

She lowered her eyes. "Spade would have any correspondence or documents relating to his business activities in his office. The only way to access the office is to use a private elevator which is locked and secured with its own security system. Even if you could get past that, which is highly unlikely, the office itself is locked and secured with its own system, and one of his goons is always lurking around. Even I don't have access to the space. No one does with the exception of Spade. Well, maybe Ace, but he is away as well. If you were hoping to let yourself in and take a look around, I'm afraid that is not going to happen. Spade is a smart man. He would never leave anything incriminating for others to find."

I supposed I should have suspected as much. "Do you know anything that might help us? Perhaps you overheard something that could point us toward the person who killed Walter Evans or Kinsley Palakiko. Or perhaps you have information about the person who kidnapped me and left me chained up in a shed on Tatsuo's estate."

Jasmine's eyes grew wide. At that moment, I knew that she did know something.

"It would help a lot if you knew anything at all," I added.

She didn't answer.

"Please."

"He is my husband. I want to send Samantha to prison, but I don't want to accomplish that by sending Spade away as well."

"I know. And I know I am asking a lot. But three people linked to Tatsuo are dead, my dad ended up in the hospital, and I was left to die in a hot shed, not to mention the countless women who have been ripped from their homes and sold to buyers in the States. I don't know if I can nail this guy, but I have to try. If Spade has been working with him, he will need to answer to that, but as long as he hasn't killed anyone…" I let the sentence dangle.

Jasmine blew out a breath and stood up. "Let's walk."

The last thing I wanted to do was walk, but I agreed and followed Jasmine as she headed toward a lush garden rich with colorful blooms.

"I honestly don't know the extent of Spade's involvement in the human trafficking enterprise," she said after a while. "As I mentioned before, Spade doesn't discuss business with me. What I do know is that he received a call on Wednesday that caused him to leave shortly after that. He never said where he'd been, but the following morning, I overheard him having a phone conversation. It sounded to me that the person on the other end of the phone was upset that Spade had handled things the way he had. At the time, I didn't have any idea who he was talking to or what he'd done wrong, but later, I overheard part of a conversation Spade had with Ace. Ace made a statement to Spade that indicated *she* was not happy."

"The *she* was probably Samantha Jones."

"Based on what you have just told me, I would assume that to be accurate."

"Do you know where Samantha is now?"

Jasmine shook her head. "I assume she might be with Spade. She does seem to weld some sort of control over him. His entire demeanor changes when she is around. Spade is a con artist and a hustler. He is very good at finding ways to make money, but the only way I can see that he would ever get involved in anything having to do with murder or human trafficking is if Samantha managed to seduce him into cooperating. The woman is bad news. She needs to be put away for a good long time."

"That is my goal as well," I confirmed. "If you hear anything that might help us find her, will you call or text me? You have my number."

"Sure. I can do that."

Jasmine rang for her goon who escorted me out of the house. I headed to my Jeep, and once I'd pulled out of the drive, I stopped to pick up Shredder.

"You heard?" I asked.

"I heard. The more I hear, the more convinced I am that Samantha Jones is behind Walter Evans' death as well as Kinsley Palakiko's death. I would be willing to bet that Spade is behind your father's stay in the hospital as well as your kidnapping. He seems to be the only bad guy involved in this little story who draws the line at murder. If I had to guess, Samantha found out that your dad provided evidence to Hoku that Kinsley was working for Tatsuo, so she sent Spade to detain the woman. Your dad showed up while Spade was there, so he knocked him out and drugged him, and then when you showed up, he did the same."

"If that were true, why did he leave Dad in the office, but transport me to the shed on Tatsuo's estate?"

Shredder frowned. "That does seem intentional."

"The person who locked me in the shed on Tatsuo's property and the person who buried Palakiko in a shallow grave on the same estate seem to be intent on chasing Tatsuo away. He isn't on the island now, so it is unlikely their intent was to have him arrested, but if he becomes a murder suspect, he will be unable to return to the island anytime soon."

"I would think Spade has a reason to want to eliminate the competition, but if he really is above killing, it couldn't have been him who killed and buried Palakiko."

"Yeah, something still isn't quite fitting," I agreed. I thought about it some more. "I feel like there is something wrong with the timeline at the Palakiko house as well."

"Yeah, I've been thinking the same thing."

"When I arrived, my dad was passed out on the floor, but I didn't see Mrs. Palakiko anywhere nor did I notice a car parked near the house other than my father's and Mrs. Palakiko's. And my dad had left hours earlier to visit Mrs. Palakiko. If he had interrupted the person sent to fetch the woman and was knocked out for his effort, why was the person who knocked him out still there to knock me out?"

"So you are thinking there were two intruders."

"It makes sense. My dad told me he was heading over to the Palakiko home about two hours before I showed up looking for him. I suppose it makes sense if the Palakiko phone was bugged, that the person who bugged the phone was made aware that we had seen Kinsley with Tatsuo and Spade. Based on what Jasmine told me, it sounds as if the person who bugged the phone, maybe Samantha, had called Spade and told him to kill or possibly detain Hoku. He shows up intent on either killing or detaining the woman, only to find that my dad is there as well. He knocks him out and then drugs him, and then takes Mrs. Palakiko to whoever had tasked him with doing so. Two hours later, I come by and find Dad, and someone else, someone who broke in later, hits me over the head and then locks me in the shed."

"That makes sense to a point, but you were drugged the same as your dad. If there were two different intruders, it makes no sense that they would have the same MO."

Shredder was right that the drug angle did seem to indicate a single intruder, but why would one guy be at the house for so long? "I feel like we should take another look around the Palakiko house. I'm sure we are missing something important. Maybe if we take another look at the scene, it will come to us."

Chapter 20

When we arrived at the Palakiko home, the first thing we noticed was a light at the back of the house. We didn't have any reason to believe that anyone was at the house, and it was possible that someone had simply left a light on, but Shredder wanted to check it out before we entered. He told me to wait by the front door while he went around to the back. I did as I was told, even though I hated being left behind. I quickly grew tired of waiting and was about to follow Shredder around to the back, when I heard a gunshot. Without even stopping to consider what I was doing, I tried the front door which was open, and let myself in. I heard a noise coming from the back of the house, so I took off down the hallway. Upon entering the kitchen, I found Shredder laying on the floor in a pool of blood. I was about to approach when I remembered my experience with my father. Instead, I paused to look around.

"Mrs. Palakiko?" I gasped, stunned to see the woman standing off to the side holding a gun.

"Why are you here? Kinsley has been found. Your job is done."

"We were hoping to find you," I answered, as I tried to wrap my head around whatever was happening. "We thought you'd been kidnapped by the same person who killed your husband." I looked at Shredder. "Why did you shoot him?"

"I didn't mean to shoot him, but he startled me and the gun just went off."

"We need to call for help. We need to get him to the hospital."

"No." Mrs. Palakiko raised her gun.

"What do you mean, no? He'll die without help." I ran forward and knelt down next to Shredder. He was bleeding heavily, but he had a pulse. I took off my shirt and shoved it over the wound. "Call 911!" I shouted."

"I said, no."

I turned slightly and looked at the woman whose hand was shaking. I could see that she was even more frightened than I was. I applied additional pressure to Shredder's wound. "I don't know what is going on, but I am not going to let my friend die. If you won't call for help, I will." I pulled my cell out of my pocket.

"I said, no!" The woman screamed, her eyes clearly communicating her panic.

I knew I was taking a chance that she would shoot me as well, but I needed to get help for Shredder, so I ignored her and hit the autodial button for Jason.

"Put the phone down," she screamed. "I don't want to hurt you, but I will if I have to."

I continued to ignore the woman. When Jason answered, I jumped right in. "I'm at the Palakiko home. Shredder has been shot. Send an ambulance."

"What are you doing?" the woman sobbed. "I said, no cops. You are going to ruin everything."

"Ruin everything? What are you talking about?"

"It should have been over. It all should have been over. Why are you here?"

Okay, this lady had definitely hopped on the crazy train at some point along the way. "What do you mean it should have been over? What should have been over?" And then I knew. Suddenly, it all made perfect sense. I increased the pressure I'd been applying to Shredder's wound. "It was you. You are the one who knocked Dad out and then when I showed up, you knocked me out as well. Why?"

"Everything went wrong. So very wrong. Samantha convinced me we had a good plan, but nothing worked out the way she said it would. Now people are dead, and I can't figure out what to do. I need time to think."

I paused to see if there was anything I should be doing for Shredder that I wasn't, but other than applying pressure to the wound, all I could do was wait for the ambulance. Hoku still had a gun pointed at us, so I decided to keep her talking. "What did Samantha talk you into doing?"

The woman used a forearm to wipe the tears from her eyes. I didn't think she was going to answer, but then she started to speak. "A woman came to the door a while back. She said her name was Samantha. She said something happened to her pilot and she needed Kinsley to do some international flights for one of her special clients. He told her no. She tried to bribe him, but he wouldn't budge, so she waited until Kinsley wasn't home and came back to talk to me. She told me that she was desperate for someone with Kinsley's unique skill set and would pay a lot of money for just a few weeks of work. We really needed the money after Kinsley gambled it all away, so I found myself agreeing to help her."

"Help her how?"

The woman let her arm drop to her side. She still clung to the gun, but at least it was no longer pointed at me. Eventually, she continued. "I spoke to Kinsley about taking the job, but he maintained his stance on the issue. I realized I wasn't getting anywhere with the stubborn mule head of a man, so I went to Samantha and told her that I'd tried, but hadn't had any more success than she had. She told me that she knew a man who she thought could help. She asked me to go along with whatever they worked out, and I unwisely agreed."

"Spade. She worked it out to have Spade help her."

Hoku nodded. "I knew about the poker game on Friday, and only acted angry that Kinsley had gone. Then when he left on Saturday, I knew that he was actually going to a private poker game, but I also knew that was part of the plan. Samantha called me on Sunday to let me know the plan had worked, and that Kinsley had agreed to the flights. She told me that Kinsley wouldn't be home for a few days, but that when he did come home, he would have enough money to pay off our debts and refill our savings. Then she called me on Monday and said that Kinsley'd had a change of heart. She said he was refusing to cooperate. She wasn't sure what was going to happen, but she wanted me to speak to him, so I met Samantha at the airstrip where Kinsley was supposed to pick up the plane he was to use. I tried to tell him just to do what he needed to do to get the money, but he was adamant that he wasn't going to transport people against their will. Samantha told me not to worry about it. She told me that she would take care of it, so I left. After I got home, I continued to stew about it. I had a bad feeling and was afraid I'd made a mistake. I really wasn't sure what was going to happen at that point, so I called your dad with the missing person story. I figured that he might be able to get Kinsley out of the mess I'd gotten him into, and even if he wasn't able to accomplish that, at least I'd have an alibi of sorts if things ended up getting ugly."

"So you knew that Samantha was going to kill Kinsley?" Wow, it really did take all kinds.

"No. I didn't know that she was going to kill him, but I knew that if he continued to refuse to cooperate, something bad would happen, and he might even turn up dead. I figured that if I reported him missing, no one would suspect me as being involved in whatever happened."

"And then?"

"And then you somehow managed to get a photo of Kinsley with Tatsuo. After your dad called me to let me know that my husband had been found, I called Samantha and told her about the photo. She was *not* happy. She told me that it was important that no one could link Tatsuo and Kinsley. She told me to kill your father when he arrived. I have a gun, and she knew it. I told her I would do what she wanted, but then once he arrived, I couldn't do it, so I hit him over the head and then drugged him. I figured that would give me time to think. I was trying to decide what to do next when you showed up. I knocked you out as well, and then called Samantha back. When she arrived, she told me that Tatsuo was going to kill her for getting things so messed up. She wanted to figure out a way to get him off her back, so she came up with the idea of chaining you up inside the shed on his property. After you'd died as a result of your ordeal, she would arrange to have you found. She figured that everyone would blame Tatsuo for your death, and that would make him a wanted man, which would cause him to avoid coming to the States, which would effectively get him off her back."

"But then I got away and messed things up."

"Exactly. She knew she needed to figure out another way to get rid of Tatsuo, so she left evidence for you to find that would lead you to Devil's Door, and she killed and buried Kinsley for you to find. She had a good plan. It should have worked. She should have had Tatsuo off her back, and I should have had the money that had been promised to me, but then you wouldn't leave well enough alone."

I could hear the sirens in the distance. I knew I just needed to stall a little longer. Shredder had lost a lot of blood, and he was unconscious, but he was still breathing.

"Did Samantha kill Walter Evans?"

"Who is Walter Evans?"

"The man she hired to pilot for Tatsuo before Kinsley. I'm pretty sure she killed him. I'm pretty sure it was inevitable that both men would die from the moment they agreed to the job flying for Tatsuo."

The woman was sobbing.

"Do you even feel a little bad that your little plan ended with the death of your husband?"

"This whole thing was his fault. If he hadn't gambled away our money, I wouldn't have had to work with Samantha in the first place."

The woman had definitely taken a turn toward the dark side. I didn't think she'd shoot me or whoever busted through the door to rescue us, but she did have the gun, and she was definitely not thinking rationally. I decided to try another tactic. "It sounds like you were the victim in this."

"I was. I shouldn't have to go to jail. I didn't mean for anyone to die. I just wanted Kinsley to earn back the money he had gambled away. None of this is really my fault."

"I agree that it was a good plan. It should have worked. If you hadn't shot Shredder, it would have worked."

The woman lifted the gun. I suppose my statement about Shredder wasn't the best move. I think I actually reminded her that she had the gun. Her eyes were wild, and her hand shook so hard I was afraid she'd accidentally pull the trigger on the dang thing whether she intended to or not.

I held out my hand. "Give me the gun."

"What? No."

"When my brother arrives, I'll tell him I shot Shredder. I'll tell him it was an accident. I'll tell him that you came down from upstairs after I'd already shot him."

"He won't believe that."

"Yes, he will. He is, after all, my brother. No one saw what really happened. Shredder probably never even saw you before the gun went off and even if he did, he's lost a lot of blood and won't remember what happened. If you give me the gun, I can make this whole mess go away." Even as I lied to the woman, I felt bad about it, but I didn't want her intentionally or accidentally shooting anyone else. I could hear the cars pull up out front. "It has to be now. Give me the gun."

Amazingly, she handed it to me. I called out when I heard the front door open. "Back here. We are in the back of the house."

As the sound of men running echoed down the hallway, I glanced at Hoku one last time. I know that it was illogical to feel remorse for the lie I had told her, but I found that I was sorry all the same. She'd made some really bad decisions, but it sounded like Samantha had managed to seduce her with money the way Jasmine felt she'd seduced Spade with her body.

Chapter 21

Tuesday, July 2

Shredder had been whisked to the hospital, Hoku had been whisked off to jail, and I had been whisked down to Jason's office to provide an official statement. I'd been covered in blood, and terrified for my friend, so the last thing I wanted to do was sit through some long interview. Jason had promised to make it brief, and then he'd promised to go to the hospital with me. In the end, I agreed to answer his questions. I told him everything I'd figured out, which took longer than I would have liked, but I hoped the information I had would be enough to put everyone involved behind bars.

By the time Jason and I arrived at the hospital, Shredder was out of surgery, but still unconscious. The doctor recommended I head home and get some rest. He assured me that there was nothing I could do and that Shredder wouldn't be conscious until the following day anyway, so while I didn't want to leave, in the end, I let Jason talk me into doing as the doctor suggested.

That was a mistake.

When returned to the hospital the next morning, Shredder was gone. I was told that someone from the government had come by and checked him out. I was assured he was being seen to and should be just fine. I knew that Shredder was considered to be some sort of a valuable asset, but it seemed a bold move for whomever he worked for to snatch him away from the hospital where he'd been admitted for treatment. As I stood dumbfounded in the waiting room of the hospital, it hit me that Shredder really was some sort of superspy. I'd suspected that for a while, but this made everything that much more real.

I had no way of getting ahold of Shredder, so all I could do was hope he'd get ahold of me. I went home and commenced with the worrying stage of this nightmare. Riptide was still with me, so I knew he'd be back, eventually.

At least Kekoa had come home last night. It was late, and she was physically and emotionally spent, so I'd decided to wait until this morning to fill her in.

"This story is so crazy as to seem completely fictional," She said as we sipped coffee on the lanai. "This whole thing started with three seemingly related deaths, and in the end, the deaths weren't related at all. I mean, what are the odds?"

"Pretty astronomical. The really crazy part is that our client turned out to be indirectly involved with murder victim number one who just happened to wash up on the beach behind the condo."

"Involved? Involved how?"

"Samantha Jones, the headhunter who provided Tatsuo with pilots for his human trafficking ring, killed both Walter Evans and Kinsley Palakiko," I reminded my cousin.

"Oh, that's right. I guess I am still trying to sort this all out. You've provided a lot of information. So the first victim, who wasn't placed for you to find, but just happened to have been found by you anyway, was a pilot the same as your missing person, and both men were hired by Samantha Jones to fly the women Tatsuo kidnapped to the States. Is she in custody?"

"She is. Jason managed to catch up with her at the airport. She was headed for Hong Kong, but I guess she must have run out of pilots since she was attempting to board a commercial flight."

"And Tatsuo?" Kekoa asked.

"He is in the wind. I doubt that anyone will catch up with him anytime soon. But at least this series of events will make it harder for him to continue to do what he has been doing. Someone will catch up with him at some point." I suspected it would be Shredder when he healed from the gunshot he received, but I still hadn't been able to speak to him, so I really had no idea what was going on with that situation.

"And Spade?"

I shrugged. "I don't know. Jason is going to interview him. I guess the whole thing will come down to proof. Spade is a careful sort of guy. There is a good chance there won't be any. I guess we'll just have to wait and see."

"I feel so bad from Jasmine," Kekoa said.

"Yeah. Me too."

Kekoa slowly shook her head. "This whole thing really is crazy. The pilot was killed by the woman who hired him, the nightclub owner was killed by a rival, and the food truck guy was killed by a man wanting to send a message to your dad. It looked as if all three murders were linked to you but it turns out that none of them really were."

"That's correct."

"You really do live a very unpredictable and odd life."

I laughed. "I guess I really do. Of course, now that you are going to be working full-time for Pope Investigations, your life is probably going to become odd and unpredictable as well. You are still going to come to work for us full-time, aren't you?"

She nodded. "I am. I had a nice visit with Cam, and I do feel like I was able to get some closure I wouldn't have if I hadn't agreed to this one last visit, but I know it's over between us. I think he knows it too. We have agreed to remain friends, but we both realize that a romantic relationship is never going to be possible as long as we live on different landmasses. He doesn't want to leave LA, and I don't want to live in LA, so breaking things off was really the only solution."

I put my hand over hers. "I'm sorry."

She shrugged. "It's okay. I'm excited about my new job with Pope Investigations, and I think I'm really ready to move on." Kekoa paused and then continued. "Any word from Luke?"

"Not really. He still says he is going to try to make a trip to the island, but it keeps getting delayed. His mom is not dealing well with the loss of her husband, and his sister is expecting another baby. I know he is torn between two worlds, but it seems obvious his family needs him more than I do. Don't get me wrong, I love Luke and wish things were different, but they aren't, and I'm honestly not sure they ever will be. I've been thinking about it, and I think I just need to call Luke and let him off the hook. He might even be relieved if I take the initiative and officially end it."

"I guess if you are really sure, then ripping off the Band-Aid might be the best move. It's really sad. The two of you were so good together, but I get it. If anyone understands what you are going through, I do. And I can say from experience, that finally making a decision, while hard, feels right."

"Yeah. I guess I'll try to call him later. I'm not sure what I am going to say, so I guess I should figure that out first." I looked at the dogs who'd been watching us chat. "I think I'm going to take the dogs down to the beach. I still can't go in the water, but my feet are on the mend, and I can throw a ball for them."

"And I think I'll unpack. Do you know when you plan to reopen Pope Investigations?"

"Dad and I plan to be at the office tomorrow. If you are feeling up to it, you can start your full-time gig then. If you need a few days, then that is fine as well."

"I'll start tomorrow. I could really use a distraction. It looks like Elva is still gone. Didn't you tell me she was supposed to be back by now?"

"Her friend decided to extend her stay by a day, but she is flying in this morning. Maybe the three of us can have dinner together."

"I'd like that."

I wanted to feel happy that the case was wrapped up, and Kekoa was home, but all I felt was empty. I supposed it was understandable that I might be sad about the way things were unfolding with Luke, and worried that I hadn't heard from Shredder. I supposed I was justified in feeling angry that people had died due to the greed of others, and sad that we hadn't managed to rescue more of the kidnapped women. But empty? I really had no explanation for empty.

Deciding to call Luke while the dogs were playing in the surf, I dialed his number.

"Lani? I wasn't expecting you to call today."

"I know. We hadn't discussed a call today, but I wanted to talk to you about something."

"Is it important? I'm sort of in the middle of something right now. I can call you back this evening."

"It can wait. Were you able to rebook your trip to Hawaii?"

"No. Things are tough right now. Maybe I can arrange to be away for a few days in the fall. I really need to run, but I will call you back."

He hung up before I could agree or even say goodbye. Luke was a good man, and I didn't blame him for the situation he found himself in, but at that moment as I stood at water's edge looking at my phone, I finally understood empty. Empty was what you were left with when hope finally died. I'd clung to the hope that Luke would find his way back to me for so long that hope had become part of my life. But now... now I was finally ready to admit that Luke returning was not going to happen. Kekoa was right; a clean break was probably the best move to make. When he called later, I'd tell him that I loved him and that I wanted us always to be friends, but I'd also tell him that I was setting him free to do what we both knew he was destined to do. It would be hard, but it was time, and I finally knew that in my heart.

"Hey, stranger."

I turned and smiled. "Shredder? What are you doing here? You should be in a hospital."

"I'm fine." Riptide came running down the beach to greet his best friend. Shredder cringed when he leaned over to greet him. "Well, maybe not fine, but I don't need to be in a hospital. I'm on leave for the next two months so my wounds can heal, and I decided to spend those two months here on the island. Once I made the decision, I couldn't wait to get home, so I checked myself out."

"That was probably a dumb move, but I am happy to see you. I've been worried. I can't believe that the people you work with checked you out of the hospital so soon after surgery."

"It's the protocol for someone who knows as much as I do. I guess my superiors don't want me talking in my sleep and giving away all their secrets."

"Do you talk in your sleep?"

"Not usually, but sometimes if I am knocked out on pain meds." Shredder turned and looked back at the condos. "I should probably sit down. Do you want to sit with me for a while? Maybe we can get whoever is around together for dinner later."

"Absolutely."

I felt that empty space in my soul fill with a tiny ray of light. Maybe hope wasn't gone. Shredder was back, Kekoa was back, Elva would be back soon, and Sean and Kevin would be home in a few days. I had a job I loved, working with a man I respected above all others, and Jason was finally starting to treat me like an equal. Maybe my life wasn't empty. Maybe it was actually pretty full, and with that realization, my world began to feel whole once again.

UP NEXT FROM KATHI DALEY BOOKS

Preview:

Rain poured down from the inky black sky as I watched Deputy Colt Wilder leverage his shovel into the saturated earth. In hindsight, it might have been a good idea to wait until after the storm had passed to check out the theory I'd been mulling around in my mind since I'd learned of Wesley Hamilton's disappearance. The heir to the Holiday Bay Community Bank had last been seen heading toward his car in the lot behind the bank ten days ago. In the days since his disappearance, no one had been able to figure out what had become of the man, and even now, all I really had to explain the fact that he seemed to have vanished into thin air, was an idea born in my imagination. An idea, I reminded myself, which was most likely nothing more than a meaningless whim based on a fantasy I'd cooked up while writing my latest novel.

"Have you found anything?" I called into the darkness, straining to be heard over the roar of the wind, rain, and occasional clap of thunder off in the distance.

"Not yet."

"Maybe we should come back another time," I suggested, as a gust of wind whipped my wet hair' across my eyes.

Colt futilely wiped the rain pouring from the brim of his hat away from his face. "You wanted to check out the gravesite, so we are checking out the gravesite. Besides, we're already soaking wet, so there is no use going back before we find what we came for."

At the time I'd made the decision to call Colt and suggest this excursion, it had seemed like a good idea. Sure, it had been raining at that point, and I knew that following through with my intuition was going to mean getting wet, but I'd lived my life in a town where it often rained, so no one could say that Abby Sullivan was afraid of a little precipitation. Of course, I'd suggested this particular course of action before the wind had blown in from the sea, causing what had seemed like a good idea at the time to end up as an act of insanity.

"I really think we should go," I tried again. "I can hear thunder off in the distance, and you are holding a metal shovel." I turned slightly to steady myself in the gale force wind.

"Hang on a minute. I might have found something."

I nodded in spite of the fact there was no way that Colt, who was standing in the hole he'd dug, would be able to see me. My breath caught as I watched Colt remove several more shovels of wet earth and set them aside.

"Well, I'll be!" He exclaimed in his deep baritone voice.

"Did you find him?"

Colt grinned in my direction. "Who would have thought that a man who had been missing for ten days would finally be found buried in his own grave."

I had to admit I was as shocked as Colt was. Sure, it was my idea to dig up the grave in the first place, but I can't say that I actually believed we'd find the guy. My suggestion that Wesley Hamilton might be buried in the gravesite reserved for him by his father before he died was really no more than a hunch. A hunch it turned out, that apparently was based in reality.

"So, what now?" I asked.

"I'm going to call in the crime scene guys before I do anything else. I need to stay here until they arrive so I won't be able to leave to take you home. Maybe Georgia can come and pick you up."

I was sure that Georgia Carter, my business partner, roommate, and best friend would be happy to come for me but I felt bad about leaving Colt standing alone in the rain, so I offered to stay. He thanked me but indicated that it might be best if I wasn't found in the immediate area when the crime scene unit arrived. I supposed he might be right so I called Georgia and then went out to the street to wait.

Georgia arrived in her beat up old truck with a travel mug of hot coffee and a warm blanket. Leave it to Georgia to think of the small touches that really did make all the difference. One of the reasons she made such a good manager for the inn we ran was because of her caring nature and attention to detail. "You look like a drowned rat," She said, after handing me the blanket. "The coffee is hot, so be careful, but a few sips should warm you right up."

"Thank you, Georgia, and thanks for coming to get me. It looks like Colt is going to be awhile."

"I can't believe Wesley Hamilton was actually buried in his own gravesite. When you suggested as much, I found the idea interesting, but I really wasn't expecting that you'd find him."

"Honestly, I am as surprised as anyone." I took a sip of the coffee. "I'm glad he has been found, but my heart is breaking for Kendall and Patrice."

Kendall Jared was Wesley's fiancée, and Patrice Hamilton was his mother. Kendall was to marry Wesley at Christmas and had been working on their wedding plans for over a year, and Patrice had recently lost her husband and was just starting to get over that loss. Losing a fiancé would be tough, but losing a son was unbearable. I should know, I'd lost mine. Sure, Johnathan had only been an infant when he was ripped out of my life by a drunk driver who had killed my husband, Ben, as well, while Wesley was well into his twenties or possibly even his early thirties, but I knew in my heart that to lose a child whatever their age could bring on the most unimaginable pain possible.

"I know this will be hard on both women," Georgia agreed, "but it seems to me that the past ten days of not knowing has to have been worse."

"Perhaps."

"I wonder who did it." Georgia turned onto the road that led to the country inn we ran together. "It seems a bold move to actually bury the guy right there in the family plot the way they did."

Georgia was right. It was bold. And actually, pretty dumb. The fact that the killer had buried Wesley in the plot reserved for him by his father indicated that he or she was someone known to Wesley and/or the Hamilton family. It didn't seem that some random tourist would even know that the Hamilton family had donated the land for the local cemetery. And it definitely didn't seem as if that same random tourist would realize that Jasper Hamilton had reserved a small corner of the land for his own family members. I bet that fact alone would narrow Colt's suspect list considerably.

"Of course," Georgia continued, bobbing her head of blond hair as she spoke, "it does seem as if Wesley had managed to make a lot of enemies during his short tenure as the bank's president. Even his own mother was pretty fed up with the way he'd been running things. The list of local businesses shut down, and families run out of their homes must be considerable by this point. I suspect it is from that list that Colt will find the killer."

"I imagine you might be right. Emotions do seem to be running high when it comes to the publics' general satisfaction with the bank. I even heard that the board of trustees had threatened to replace Wesley as president if he didn't harness his Scrooge-like tendencies just a bit."

"Could they do that? Replace Wesley? His father established the bank, and he did leave it to his only son."

"I don't know the specifics, but the bank does have stockholders, and even though Wesley owned a majority share, the bank also has a board of trustees that seems to weld a certain amount of power. The rumor circulating around town about the board threatening to replace Wesley may be nothing more than a rumor, but in my mind, the very idea of having anyone other than a Hamilton at the helm seems to indicate just how unhappy everyone is."

"I suppose it wouldn't hurt to start a list of those residents we know of who have been negatively impacted by the bank's new policies," Georgia commented, as she parked in front of our seaside cottage.

Once we arrived home, I headed inside to take a hot shower while Georgia made a pot of tea. Since the inn had opened, we'd settled into the routine of sharing a pot of tea and discussing the comings and goings at the inn at the end of each day. Georgia was in charge of the day-to-day operations, but I owned the place and wanted to stay in the loop, so the routine had developed naturally.

As I shampooed my hair, I thought about the body in the cemetery. The idea to check out Wesley's gravesite had come about as a result of the thriller I was currently working on. In my fictional story featuring an agent from the FBI who'd teamed up with a psychic to find a serial killer, the body of one of the victims had eventually been found in a cemetery. As I wrote this passage, the idea of checking our cemetery for Wesley's remains took hold. The fact that he actually had been buried there was surprising even to me.

"I have pumpkin cookies to go with the tea," Georgia informed me after I'd emerged from my bedroom wearing my pajamas and a warm robe.

"Tea and cookies sound perfect." I curled up on the sofa after setting my teacup on the table in front of me. Georgia's dog, Ramos, and my dog, Molly, were curled up in front of the fire, but my cat, Rufus, jumped up onto the sofa and curled up in my lap. "So who checked in and who checked out, and what do we know about the new arrivals?"

"The Osgood's checked out of suite one today," Georgia started. While we'd named all the suites, we'd also numbered them for simplicities sake with one being the suite on the first floor, two and three on the second, four and five on the third, and leaving the attic suite as six. "We don't have anyone arriving for that suite until the Goodmans check in on Thursday. A woman named Dixie Highlander checked in today with her daughter, Holly. They are occupying suites two and three. They plan to be here for two weeks."

"I'm assuming Holly is an adult daughter?"

"She is. I would say that Holly is probably in her mid-twenties, and Dixie is probably around fifty. Maybe fifty-five. It's hard to tell. The women seem very nice, and they actually have an interesting reason for being here."

I took a sip of my tea, allowing the warmth to glide slowly down my throat. "Oh, and what's that?"

Georgia crossed her legs under her body and leaned forward slightly. "Dixie was put up for adoption when she was four years old. She told me that she didn't remember much about her birth parents and never spent much time thinking about them once she had gone onto her new home. In fact, according to Dixie, by the time she was an adult, she couldn't even remember their names or what they'd looked like. But a few months ago, she received a small package in the mail. The package contained a handwritten letter from a woman who identified herself only as R and a leather-bound journal. R stated in her letter than she'd been a friend of Dixie's birth mother, and that she wanted to both inform Dixie of her mother's death and to send along the only thing she had of hers, which apparently was an old journal that her mother had kept at around the time Dixie was born. She didn't know if Dixie was interested or if she had questions about her birth and eventual adoption, but she indicated in the letter that, if she did, the journal should help with that."

"I wonder how the friend got the journal in the first place," I said. "Actually, I'm even more interested in how the friend knew how to get ahold of Dixie if she had been given up for adoption all those years ago."

"I don't know. Dixie didn't know, but she was curious, so she read the journal. As it turns out, Dixie is one of four children. She was the oldest, and if the journal is accurate, she had three sisters: twins, Hannah and Heather, who'd been two when their mother surrendered custody, and an infant named Lily."

"Wow. That's some story. Is Dixie here to try to find her sisters?"

"She is, although she has very little to go on. The person who sent the journal didn't include a mailing address, but the postmark on the package is from the post office here in Holiday Bay, so she, along with her daughter, decided to visit the area and see what they could dig up."

"If Dixie was four when her mother gave up custody of her children, she must remember something."

"She said she had just turned four when she went to her new home, and she really hadn't remembered a thing about her life before that until she received the package with the journal. But since then, small snippets have come to her. She is pretty sure her mother had dark hair, and she thinks they lived in a forested area. She doesn't remember having a father, but she does remember the twins and the baby. She told me that her memories are really disjoined and she isn't even certain if what she thinks she remembers is an actual memory or simply a fake memory born in her imagination."

I picked up a cookie and took a bite. "I get that. I sometimes have memories that feel very real to me, but my sister insists that the events I swear I remember from our childhood, never happened. I remember living in a house with a grand entry, but Annie and I went through every house we ever lived in as children, and none of them had a grand entry."

"I suppose the remnants of dreams and fantasies exist in our minds the same way memories of actual events do. Once the image is planted, I can see how the two might get mixed up."

I took a sip of my tea. "I will admit that Dixie's story has caught my attention. I'll have to make a point of introducing myself at breakfast. Did Dixie indicate whether the journal mentioned why their mother put them up for adoption?"

"According to the journal, her mother became ill and thought she was going to die. She was no longer able to care for her children on her own, and the father of her children had taken off when he'd found out she was pregnant with baby number four, so she decided that adopting them out was her only option. Since R indicated in the letter she sent that Dixie's mother had recently died, I guess we can assume she must not have died from the illness which caused her to give up her children. Of course, she never sought them out, so I guess she must have assumed they were better off in their new homes."

"I can't imagine being faced with that choice. I wonder if Dixie's mother had any family she could have gone to."

"It seems that she must not have or perhaps her family was unwilling to take on four little girls. It's hard to understand why the mother made the choice she did without having all of the pieces to the puzzle."

Rufus jumped down off my lap and joined the dogs by the fire. I supposed I was moving around too much for his liking. It was just as well. It was tricky to balance hot tea and cookies with a twenty-five pound cat in your lap. "So did the man who planned to check into suite four arrive?" I asked, changing the subject back to a review of the day.

"He did. He is in the area for a job interview, so he only plans to stay three nights, but we have a young couple checking into that room for the weekend, so the suite will only be vacant two nights. A man and his niece checked into suite five today. I didn't have a chance to speak with them at length, but I sense there is a story there as well. And, of course, Gaylord is still in the attic suite."

Gaylord Godfry was a retired history professor who'd checked into the inn three weeks ago. He'd told us that he planned to use his time in Maine to write the great American novel. I had no idea if he was a talented writer, but he did seem to be putting in the time required to write a novel. His reservation was open-ended, which worked out good for us, and we were happy to have him.

"Did Gaylord decide if he wanted to participate in the murder mystery dinner party? It's just two weeks away, and the company that puts on the event wants to get a final headcount."

"I'll ask him tomorrow," Georgia said. "We have all six suites booked for that weekend, and the guests from the other five suites have confirmed their reservation to attend the party. We also have about twenty people from town who have reserved spots. If Gaylord decides to join us, we should have an even thirty, which puts us at capacity. The thirty is not counting you and me, or Nikki, but I figured we'd all be working the event and wouldn't join in."

Nikki Peyton lived with her brother, Tanner Peyton, on the estate to the north of us. Tanner trained dogs for service organizations, and Nikki, his much younger half-sister, helped Georgia with cleaning and laundry at the inn.

"And the pumpkins for the pumpkin patch?"

"They will arrive on Friday of this week. We will need to get them placed on the lawn once they show up. I've been advertising for weeks that we will have music on the lawn, crafts for sale from local craftsmen, and pumpkins and face painting for the kids both Saturday and Sunday. The inn looks fantastic, and I think this is a good opportunity to show off what we have accomplished and what we have to offer."

"I agreed. I'm looking forward to the entire month. Did Lonnie come by and help you hang the skeletons in the hallways?"

Georgia nodded. Lonnie Parker had been hired to oversee the renovation of the inn, and even though his job was now complete, we could always count on him to come by when we needed some muscle or some height since Georgia and I were both petite.

"While he was here, he mentioned that he would be by this week to check out the flicker we seem to be having with the lights in the gazebo."

I smiled. "The flicker that Gaylord is certain is linked to the strange noises he's been hearing in the hallways at night?"

Georgia's face grew serious. "I realize that Gaylord's assertion that we have spooks living in the house is sort of out there, but he's not the only guest to mention the rattling in the hallway. The couple who checked out of suite two a few days ago swore they heard a pitter-patter overhead, and the man who stayed in suite three, said he felt a presence when he got up to grab a snack in the middle of the night."

"It's probably just the very realistic decorations you've put out. We wanted to create the feel of a haunted inn, and apparently, we've done just that."

"What about the flickering lights in the gazebo?" Georgia asked.

"I'm sure it is just a short in the wiring system. The lights inside the house haven't been flickering have they?"

"Not that I know of." Georgia got up and walked to the window. It was still pouring rain. "I guess I should go and do our nighttime lockdown." She pulled on a rain slicker. "Hopefully, if we do have a ghost, it will behave itself tonight."

The inn was a twenty-four hour a day undertaking. Georgia and I had established a routine of locking all the doors and making sure all the overhead lights on the main floor were off at ten. There were dim nightlights for guests who might get up for a drink or a snack after ten, and all the suite keys also opened the back door leading from the kitchen out to the drive between the house and cottage should one of the guests return from town after lockup. At this point, Georgia was working seven days a week with Nikki's help, but eventually, we planned to employ someone to cover the daily operations at least one day a week so Georgia could have some time off. Of course, we'd only just begun booking rooms two months ago, so in the short term, Georgia seemed fine with the way things were. She provided a hot breakfast and dinner, but the guests were on their own for lunch. Nikki helped with the cleaning and laundry, which freed Georgia up to focus on marketing, reservations, and the food.

I picked up my teacup and cookie plate and set them in the sink, and then began emptying the dishwasher. During the day, Georgia handled the inn while I focused on my writing, and we generally shared the chores associated with the cottage we shared, but now Georgia had a full-time job the same as me. Now that my writing career had taken off and the inn was open, Georgia and I were both busier than we first imagined we would be. It was fine, though. I could see that Georgia was in her element with meals to prepare and guests to see to, and I was happy to be back in the saddle in the publishing industry. I'd started off slowly, uncertain of my readiness to be back in the public eye, but I had a book signing tomorrow at the local bookstore, and my newest novel would be released next month.

I reached up to place a pair of wine glasses on the overhead rack when I noticed that I had a call. It was Colt, so I picked up. "Hey. So what's going on? Did the body we found belong to Wesley Hamilton?"

"It did. At least the first one."

"First one?"

"Once the crime scene guys got here and excavated Wesley's body, we found another body beneath his."

"You're kidding?"

"I'm afraid not. The body beneath Wesley's is fully decayed, so at this point, I don't know who it belonged to or how long it's been there. What I do know is that whoever killed Wesley was not the first one to have the idea to bury their kill in the Hamilton family plot."

Books by Kathi Daley
Come for the murder, stay for the romance.

Zoe Donovan Cozy Mystery:
Halloween Hijinks
The Trouble With Turkeys
Christmas Crazy
Cupid's Curse
Big Bunny Bump-off
Beach Blanket Barbie
Maui Madness
Derby Divas
Haunted Hamlet
Turkeys, Tuxes, and Tabbies
Christmas Cozy
Alaskan Alliance
Matrimony Meltdown
Soul Surrender
Heavenly Honeymoon
Hopscotch Homicide
Ghostly Graveyard
Santa Sleuth
Shamrock Shenanigans
Kitten Kaboodle
Costume Catastrophe
Candy Cane Caper
Holiday Hangover
Easter Escapade
Camp Carter
Trick or Treason
Reindeer Roundup
Hippity Hoppity Homicide
Firework Fiasco

Henderson House
Holiday Hostage
Lunacy Lake
Celtic Christmas – *December 2019*

Zimmerman Academy The New Normal
Zimmerman Academy New Beginnings
Ashton Falls Cozy Cookbook

Tj Jensen Paradise Lake Mystery:
Pumpkins in Paradise
Snowmen in Paradise
Bikinis in Paradise
Christmas in Paradise
Puppies in Paradise
Halloween in Paradise
Treasure in Paradise
Fireworks in Paradise
Beaches in Paradise
Thanksgiving in Paradise – *October 2019*

Rescue Alaska Mystery:
Finding Justice
Finding Answers
Finding Courage
Finding Christmas
Finding Shelter – *Early 2020*

Whales and Tails Cozy Mystery:

Romeow and Juliet
The Mad Catter
Grimm's Furry Tail
Much Ado About Felines
Legend of Tabby Hollow
Cat of Christmas Past
A Tale of Two Tabbies
The Great Catsby
Count Catula
The Cat of Christmas Present
A Winter's Tail
The Taming of the Tabby
Frankencat
The Cat of Christmas Future
Farewell to Felines
A Whisker in Time
The Catsgiving Feast
A Whale of a Tail
The Catnap Before Christmas – *December 2019*

Writers' Retreat Mystery:

First Case
Second Look
Third Strike
Fourth Victim
Fifth Night
Sixth Cabin
Seventh Chapter
Eighth Witness
Ninth Grave

A Tess and Tilly Mystery:
The Christmas Letter
The Valentine Mystery
The Mother's Day Mishap
The Halloween House
The Thanksgiving Trip
The Saint Paddy's Promise
The Halloween Haunting – *September 2019*

The Inn at Holiday Bay:
Boxes in the Basement
Letters in the Library
Message in the Mantel
Answers in the Attic
Haunting in the Hallway – *August 2019*
Pilgrim in the Parlor – *October 2019*
Note in the Nutcracker – *December 2019*

The Hathaway Sisters:
Harper
Harlow
Hayden – *Early 2020*

Haunting by the Sea:
Homecoming by the Sea
Secrets by the Sea
Missing by the Sea
Betrayal by the Sea
Christmas by the Sea – *Fall 2019*
Thanksgiving by the Sea – *Fall 2020*

Sand and Sea Hawaiian Mystery:

Murder at Dolphin Bay
Murder at Sunrise Beach
Murder at the Witching Hour
Murder at Christmas
Murder at Turtle Cove
Murder at Water's Edge
Murder at Midnight
Murder at Pope Investigations
Murder at Shell Beach - *Early 2020*

A Cat in the Attic Mystery:

The Curse of Hollister House – *September 2019*
The Mystery Before Christmas – *November 2019*

Seacliff High Mystery:

The Secret
The Curse
The Relic
The Conspiracy
The Grudge
The Shadow
The Haunting

Road to Christmas Romance:

Road to Christmas Past

USA Today best-selling author Kathi Daley lives in beautiful Lake Tahoe with her husband Ken. When she isn't writing, she likes spending time hiking the miles of desolate trails surrounding her home. She has authored more than a hundred books in eleven series, including Zoe Donovan Cozy Mysteries, Whales and Tails Island Mysteries, Tess and Tilly Cozy Mysteries, Sand and Sea Hawaiian Mysteries, Tj Jensen Paradise Lake Series, Inn at Holiday Bay Cozy Mysteries, Writers' Retreat Southern Seashore Mysteries, Rescue Alaska Paranormal Mysteries, Haunting by the Sea Paranormal Mysteries, Family Ties Mystery Romances, and Seacliff High Teen Mysteries. Find out more about her books at www.kathidaley.com

Stay up-to-date:
Newsletter, *The Daley Weekly* http://eepurl.com/NRPDf
Webpage – www.kathidaley.com
Facebook at Kathi Daley Books – www.facebook.com/kathidaleybooks
Kathi Daley Books Group Page – https://www.facebook.com/groups/569578823146850/
E-mail – kathidaley@kathidaley.com
Twitter at Kathi Daley@kathidaley – https://twitter.com/kathidaley
Amazon Author Page – https://www.amazon.com/author/kathidaley
BookBub – https://www.bookbub.com/authors/kathi-daley

South Lake Tahoe

44724021R00120

Made in the USA
San Bernardino, CA
21 July 2019